being human
Bad Blood

being human

BAD BLOOD

James Goss

Being Human is a Touchpaper TV production for BBC Three
Executive Producers: Toby Whithouse and Rob Pursey

Original series created by Toby Whithouse and broadcast on BBC Television.
'Being Human' and the Being Human logo are trademarks of the
British Broadcasting Corporation and are used under licence

10 9 8 7 6 5 4 3 2 1

Published in 2010 by BBC Books, an imprint of Ebury Publishing.
A Random House Group Company.

The Random House Group Ltd Reg. No. 954009.
Addresses for companies within the Random House Group can be found at
www.randomhouse.co.uk.

A CIP catalogue record for this book is available from the British Library.

ISBN 978 1 846 07900 9

The Random House Group Limited supports the Forest Stewardship Council
(FSC), the leading international forest certification organisation. All our titles
that are printed on Greenpeace approved FSC certified paper carry the FSC
logo. Our paper procurement policy can be found at www.rbooks.co.uk/
environment

Series Editor: Steve Tribe
Cover design by Lee Binding © Woodlands Books, 2010

Printed and bound in Great Britain by CPI Cox and Wyman, Reading, RG1 8EX

To buy books by your favourite authors and register for offers,
visit www.rbooks.co.uk

Gather ye rosebuds while ye may,
Old Time is still a-flying,
And this same flower that smiles to-day
To-morrow will be dying.
Robert Herrick, *To the Virgins to Make Much of Time*

EYES DOWN FOR A FULL HOUSE

I wake up. I'm in a house. Someone else's house. Comfortable, but a bit studenty. You know — cushions and throws and fairy lights. Hi-fi and telly front-and-centre, so you can tell boys live here — but also quite tidy, so I'm guessing at least one woman. Oh yeah, this would have to be a shared house. That would be it — hope the poor cow isn't on her own, trying to keep order in a house full of boys. There's probably a rota of some sort. Yeah, bet there's a rota.

Ow. Something hurts.

The pain's odd. Like it's not really there. But it's quite massive.

Hangover? No. Not really. Hmm.

Oh, there's a cup of tea on the table by me. That's nice. If only I could reach it. But my arm can't quite seem to… come on, arm… no, it's not moving. Wake up, girl. Look around. You've woken up in worse places. Remember that balcony on Mykonos.

There's an old black and white film on the telly. One of those things I've never really seen the point of – you know, thirty-six coppers leap quickly into a van which drives off, tipping them all out, and they get up and run after it, truncheons waving to a frantically tinkling piano. Love that tinkling piano. If my life ever gets a soundtrack, that's what I'd like for it. Plinky Plink Plonk! Plinky Plink Plonk!

My eyes can't really focus on the film. I try frowning but it's not really helping things much. Wonder if I can change the channel. Where's the remote? Bet it's mid-morning by now – must be time for Loose Women. *Wonder if John Barrowman's on?*

My eyes drift across the room. I can't really control them, they're spinning a little – you know that magic rollover vision you get when you go to bed with a skinful? Yeah, like that. Your bed turns into a ship in a storm, and you're clinging on to the side and wondering whether you're going to fall out or throw up.

Actually, yeah, thanks for asking, I do feel a bit sick. Maybe it's going to be one of those hangovers. Lovely. Better scope out the bathroom, or at least a sink. You classy girl, Denise.

And then I see her – she's leaning over me (why haven't I noticed her before?) and she's wearing pyjamas. Probably wondering who the trash is and how to get rid of her before she has to go off to work. Actually... she's really young, great skin, brilliantly curly hair, worried expression. She puts down another cup of tea by the one I've got already. And she smiles – it's a tiny, sad little smile. And I know her! I'm sure I do. Of course, it's –

My eyes drift down and to the left, and there on the floor is a man, sitting cross-legged like a kid. He's a proper 'meet you in the bar on the first night, bang you senseless and then smirk at you as he neatly avoids you for the rest of the holiday' bastard. His hands are sweeping through his hair, and he's staring at me. It's quite disconcerting actually. He's really, really looking at me... hungrily, almost through me. As though he can see my thoughts.

Then there's a banging noise, and my eyes slide right (sickeningly, eurgh!) – and there's a third guy. He's nervous, very nervous – and the panic suits him. He's got a face made for worrying. And he's got his back to the door, spread across it as though it's being beaten down, and he's gripping the frame tightly and he's sweating frantically. He's screaming. And he's looking at me, and he's looking at the guy on the floor, and he's looking at the girl, and then he's looking back at me, and he's screaming at us to help him.

I can't hear his voice, but I can read his lips. 'They're coming! They're coming!' he's crying. And the door is being pushed open behind him, and his fingers are losing their grip on the door frame...

And I can't move. I wish I could help him, but I can't move. And then my eyes spin around the room – at the frantic boy, at the hungry man, at the sad-eyed girl. And then my eyes roll up and settle on the drip feeding into my arm.

And then I remember...

CUP OF TEA

23

Denise

Well, I guess I said the wrong thing right at the start:

'Hi! Is Owen there?'

The guy behind the door stares at me, his mouth wide open and making little gulps like a dying fish. He takes his glasses off and wipes them on his sleeve.

'N-no,' he breathes eventually, looking as innocent as Fred West buying cement, 'Noooooo. He's not here. Nope.' He's kind of cute in a shoplifting Boy Scout way.

'Right then,' I say. 'Will he be back soon?'

The man shakes his head, his jowls flying loose. 'No, not imminently. Why, would you like to leave a message?' He gulps. 'N-not that that would be a good idea. Not a great idea at all. He probably won't read it. Er...' And his voice rises like he's caught something personal in his zipper.

The door is flung open more widely and another man

11

appears. He's… predatory. Yeah, that's a good word. He's a really good-looking mess of cheekbones and sideburns and brooding eyes and a sexily bored expression that takes in his friend and me and then, I can just tell, mentally undresses me. Slowly.

'Hi,' he says. The other man gives a yelp of grateful relief. 'Can we help you?'

I match him eyeball for eyeball, and I smile. 'Hello, gorgeous!' I say. 'I'm Denise, friend of Owen's. Where is the filthy swine?'

'Owen?' The man smiles back at me. Nice teeth. 'No. He's not here. Sorry.' And he makes to close the door.

'What about Annie?' I ask.

The door swings back open.

'Annie?'

I step in, talking as I walk. This isn't what I was expecting. 'Well, I see it's not changed much since the last time I was here,' I say.

'Excuse me?' says Predator. Oh, he's shocked, but he's found time to sweep the hair out of his eyes and stick his hands in his pockets before slouching against a wall. I'm getting tired of him.

His friend is bounding around us like an agitated guppy. He's trying to whisper: 'She! Has! Been! Here! Before!' It's as subtle as skywriting, but kind of cute. Gawd, I hope he's not a primary school teacher – he'd last about a minute.

I fold my arms. 'Owen and Annie,' I say firmly. 'Friends from uni. They lived here, last time I looked. Lovely couple. Were getting married. They still live here? Or have you two men killed and eaten them?'

'Eaten!' gasps the boy, and probably lets out a little bit of wee.

The Predator just looks at me and smiles quietly. Sizing me up.

There is a cough, and I turn.

'Annie!' I laugh. 'Oh, it's good to see you!'

Annie

She can see me! No one else can, but Denise O'Bloody O'Halloran can see me! She's back! And she can see me! Of course, if anyone could see me, it'd be her. Great. Just great. Everyone Loves Denise standing in my living room.

How long has it been? Two years maybe. And she's looking good. Good as she ever does. Funny that. Some people get changed by the world, but oh no, not her. She just looks – no, seasoned isn't the word, is it? But she's got a proper tan on her – not like Julie Tango-Face, but a real rich deep-bake, like the colour of wood in a stately home. And she's as thin as ever, in really tight jeans. And they're looking really good on her.

Which is slightly annoying. It's comfy, honestly, wearing these clothes day-in day-out, but it would be nice to wear something a bit more…

She looks as bothered by the world at large as ever. It's a grey day outside, it's raining, it's a bit of a write-off, but she doesn't care. She's smiling. She's got the measure of George and Mitchell without even blinking, and she's looking at me. She always could do that thing… maddening. What do I say? She's probably just dropping by. Hey. Company is good. And she can see me! Result! That's got to be a good thing. I was beginning to wonder if it was just going to be George and Mitchell for ever from now on.

'Hello, Denise,' I say. 'It's so good to see you.' I mean it. I step forward and I smile. 'Fancy a cup of tea?'

'Great,' mutters George and I see him roll his eyes – 'Here we go again.' But I look at him and he freezes.

Mitchell comes bounding over. 'Tea! Lovely idea!' he says. 'I'll pop the kettle on!' He rubs his hands. Oh God. He's in one of his genial moods.

'Tea? What's wrong with vodka?' laughs Denise, 'Oh Annie, you haven't changed a bit.'

Oh, this is going to be difficult. But it's Denise. It'll be fine.

'And you're the same as ever!' I say, wondering if I dare risk a matey shoulder punch. Best not to – don't know if I'm real enough to –

She hugs me! And I don't vanish. I don't end up falling through a friend from university. We just hug. I can feel her and I can smell her – she's wrapped around me and I get a really strong whiff of good conditioner (the boys just don't get it), and I try not to cling on for dear life as it feels so nice. She thinks I'm real. She thinks I'm alive. She feels… oh, she feels so good.

She steps back, a little puzzled beneath it all. 'Ooh, you're a bit cold, Annie luv,' she says, rubbing my arms.

'Oh,' I say, managing an actual nonchalant shrug, thank you very much, 'it's the central heating in this place. Owen never got it working properly.' And, with a gesture, I suggest that that's why I'm wearing comfy clothes.

'So, Owen not around?' she says, eyes narrowing. Oh damn you, Denise. I was enjoying this.

'He's, ah, moved out…' I say. Well, probably locked up in a padded cell after I drove him mad for murdering me, but there's such a thing as Too Much Detail in small talk.

'Oh.' Her mouth moves a little. 'Really?' She steps forward, and it's like she's no longer wearing make-up. Her face falls, and she pats my shoulder (and I can still feel it! Brilliant!). 'Sorry about that, luv. You guys were great… Sorry…' She knows just what to say – not sweeping it under the carpet, not gushing. Just nice.

'Yeah,' I say. 'Moving on. You know. It was a while ago. This is George.'

'Heeeeelloooooooooo,' he says uneasily, smiling at her then making frantic *get rid of her* gestures when she turns away.

'And my kitchen slave is Mitchell.'

'Hey!' comes through the doorway along with a rattling of mugs.

Denise nods, approving. 'Two good-looking boys,' she says, fixing George with a beam that makes him squirm. 'Way to move on, girl. Which one's every day and which one's Sunday Best?'

'Oh no,' sighs George. 'I'm not Sundays.'

'Sweet,' laughs Denise, taking a cup of tea from Mitchell as he pads softly through. He leans back against the bookshelf and sips from his mug, quietly amused and wary.

'These guys are just around to cover the mortgage,' I say.

'Take you to the pub, shoulder to cry on, all that stuff, yeah,' says Denise. 'Good for you! Last time I got dumped, I swear I nearly got a cat. And that's like giving in, I say. You may as well just slump around wearing yesterday's make-up and last night's pyjamas.'

I cough, and gather my clothes around me.

Denise smiles, and she's understanding. 'I'm the last thing you need, aren't I? Turning up to remind you of that past life. Gassing on like nobody's business about old times and all that. God, look at me! I'm so sorry. I should really just leave, right now, get out of your hair, go, vamoose, skedaddle, never look back.' She settles down on the sofa.

'No!' I know she's not serious. 'No, God no, don't go. Come on. Let's catch up, since you're in the area. Er – why are you in the area?'

Denise waves the question away. 'Oh, I'm back in the country for a bit. Look at the old sights, knock hell out of a few old friends, break a few hearts, nick some money off Dad. It's been ages since I've been in Blighty. A year at least – I've been travelling.'

'Look at you!' I say, impressed. 'It suits you.'

And it does. Denise is one of those people who's larger than life. Stupid expression isn't it? It normally means 'slightly dumpy girl with lots of gay friends', but Denise isn't – oh, she's never going to be a size zero, but it's always looked good on her. And she's so bloody healthy – tanned skin glowing, and she's showing so much cleavage that Mitchell and George are titnotised.

'What about you?' she asks. 'Up to much? You always did have grand plans. I bet it's something dead good.'

'Oh…' Damn. 'Well, I was… you know, working in the hospitality industry.'

'Pub down the road,' whispers Mitchell.

'Yes, *thank you*, Mitchell,' I say. 'But you know – taking a break from all that at the moment.'

Denise nods and smiles, taking a sip from her tea. 'Working in a pub? It's a laugh, though, and I bet you stole all the crisps. I know I would.'

'Yeah,' I say, trying to seem truthful.

Denise settles back in the sofa and smoothes her jeans down. As she leans over, I can see Mitchell craning forward for another peep at her assets. She looks up, and beams at him. 'Have you got any biccies, luv?'

'George has got some HobNobs,' offers Mitchell, smiling.

'Oh. I'll just go and get them, shall I?' says George, shooting Mitchell a poisonous glance as he slouches off to the kitchen.

So we sit there. There's a little plate of biscuits in the middle of the room, and we're all gathered loosely round them. Nodding a little and saying less. This is Denise. I'm dying to tell her I'm dead. Because if anyone would understand, it's Denise. That's how she was at uni. I remember there was that time I thought Owen and I had split up for good and I just sat up all night until there was a good time to tap on her door. Finally at half five I knocked, and of course she was there, pushing the sleep out of her eyes and waving me in. And she was like the best friend I'd ever had, and I was also pleased because a tiny, nasty bit of me had wondered if Owen would be in there. That would have killed me. Seeing her in her giant Kinks T-shirt and him in a pair of boxers and that look on his face. That fuck off and die look. Which, of course, he meant literally.

But no. He wasn't there. It was just Denise that morning. She'd run out of tea and coffee, so we sat in her bed, drinking Cup-a-Soup and watching the sun rise.

Sometimes... oh sometimes she was so nice I hated her, just a little. Nothing ever got to her, she never bothered with diets or hangovers. 'Life's too short for that, isn't it?' she'd say, and she'd look at me and wink. It's like she knew...

I want to tell her. I want to tell her I'm dead, right now. Really I do. But it's like the only secret I've got. So we sit. And we're a bit silent. Not quite an awkward silence, but not quite that comfortable silence between old friends.

'Lovely tea, Mitchell,' she says, giving him a little smile. She takes the last biscuit, George watching her like a sullen dog. Not a proper big dog, but one of those tiny little fit-in-a-handbag dogs.

'So why didn't you come to my funeral?' I want to ask.

But no.

'Where've you been?'

That's waaaay safer.

Denise leans back and laughs. Laughs like she's having the most fun. 'Holiday rep. Isles of Greece. All over. Time of my life. Went out for a month, haven't been back for two years. Sun, sea, sand and all the rest.' She laughs again. 'My god, Annie – you should do it. You'd love it. Making new friends every week, lots of parties, lots of men who don't hang around long enough to break your heart, Greek cheese, kipping in the afternoon on a sun-lounger. Ohhhh…' She grins.

That explains it, really. That's Denise all over. She's never been the quiet-night-in sort, never stood still. Always up and about and moving on. Always somehow at lectures and then sport and then dinner and then the cinema and then the pub and then let's go on somewhere… 'You're a long time dead,' she'd laugh.

Ain't that the truth?

George

Why'd Annie have to do that? Why'd she suddenly have to appear? Couldn't she for once just keep it simple, eh? Is that too much to ask? Well, obviously, yes, it is. Oh, that's just typical. Marvellous. We have plenty on our plate at the moment, thank you very much, and I really do feel that we could do with just a little moment, a nice little moment to sit down and really think things through. And do we get that? No, we do not.

Because, you know – after all that 'no one else can see me any more' – all of a sudden, she has to pop up in front of this woman. Having your cake and eating your cake, that's what it is. Not that we've got any cake.

Oh no. Being invisible, that would have been too easy, wouldn't it? Denise could have turned up, we could have said, 'No, sorry, Owen's moved out. Sorry you missed him. Have a nice life.' Shut the door, and it would have been over in under a minute. Back to reality. But no. Let's go for complex.

So instead, Annie and Owen's oldest, bestest friend is having tea with a ghost, and we're sat around praying it doesn't go horribly wrong. I don't know how Mitchell's handling it, but I'm terrified. I am. This is so awkward.

Sending Denise away. 'Sorry, she's dead. Bye.' Well, it wouldn't have even been lying really, would it? I mean, Annie is actually dead. That's not just a technicality, that's the truth. I'm sorry, but it is. And my family always said that telling the truth was the easiest thing.

And it is. I mean, clearly not the whole truth. That would be silly. But most of the truth, certainly. She doesn't need to know that Owen's a murdering nutter, and his ex fiancée is a ghost who's now living with a vampire and a werewolf. Just enough truth to get her to go away.

But now look at this. Oh yeah – to you it may look like tea and biscuits (*my* biscuits), but it's the start of a truth meltdown of nuclear proportions. Cos we're all sat here. What if Denise isn't just on a flying visit, passing through like a tikka masala? What if she bumps into another old friend? 'Saw Annie, she looks well,' she'll say. 'Oh really?'

they'll say. 'I heard she's dead.'

Yeah, that'll work wonderfully. Marvellous.

So we're all going to pretend that we're not sat on a time bomb. Not that time bombs have seats. Certainly not seats with cushions. Oh, George, you're rambling and of course you're just obsessing because she's just eaten the last biscuit.

There were seven biscuits left in that packet. I was saving them. Because Nina bought them. Every time I'd eat a biscuit, there'd be a little bit less Nina in the house. And I was saving them. And now there's none left. I don't know precisely what percentage of Nina that packet of HobNobs represented – I mean, all in all, we're talking a couple of towels, toothbrush, lip salve and a book, but if you look at it like that, in terms of volume, then half a packet of biscuits would be like ten per cent. So yes, there's now ten per cent less Nina. Thanks, new girl.

But you know what? If it makes Annie happy, then it's worth it. Denise can see her. And that's something. I was starting to worry that she was just fading away. But she can be seen by someone else. So maybe if we can just get through a cup of tea and some chit-chat and maybe, just for once, the worst thing won't happen? Eh? Because that would be very nice for a change.

Then this Denise, she puts down her tea, and she laughs, and she says, 'Come on then, let's go out and have a proper drink!'

Oh no.

Mitchell

Oh, I don't care. She's really good looking, she makes Annie smile, and she smells lovely. Plus, she gets me. I know she gets me. And she rattles George. Bless George. He's doing that thing he does around pretty women. It's like he's a shopping trolley with a broken wheel, going round and round and round, bumping into things and squeaking really, really loudly.

Round and round and round. Squeak. Squeak. Squeak.

There was this house. Kids' bedroom. Stars glowing on the ceiling. And I stood there. Hungry. Can't remember why I was there. But there I was. And these two kids. Asleep. Necks on the pillows.

Round and round and round. Squeak. Squeak. Squeak.

The hunger rushed up, pounding away. And, if I blinked, that would be it. Don't blink, don't blink, don't blink. Just get out. But there was the hunger, and there were those necks.

Blood is like wine. Some vampires say that to try and make it sound all exciting, and they're lying, kind of. At the start you think it's rubbish, you know, dressing up a thirst for a body fluid as some kind of art form. Like they'd bother to do the same thing if vampires fed off saliva: 'Oh yes, what a cheeky little phlegm.' No, somehow with blood it's suddenly all that bollocks about the velvety attack and the oaky finish, and traffic warden's great for barbeques, all sorts of stuff copied off of labels. And you know, it's a silly thing to say.

Round and round and round. Squeak. Squeak. Squeak.

But it's not a complete lie. Blood tastes different. Smells different. George, for instance. I'd never tell him, but he reeks. Like old stables. That's why vampires really don't go for werewolves – the smell is just wrong. Every now and then I'll notice it. Savour it accidentally. I'd be sick if I still could be. But most of the time I don't notice it. And because

I've stopped noticing it on George, I've stopped noticing it so much on people. They naturally smell so good. Good enough to eat. Like bacon frying. I mean, Denise – she smells really nice. And that smell never goes away. But, if you try, it fades into the background.

But some smells you just can't ignore. And there I am. Back in that bedroom with two children. And, if you're trying to be impressive, they're what'd you'd call an audacious young Beaujolais. That beautiful not-yet-ripe blood mixed with the smell of milk. It's irresistible. Creamy and sweet.

Round and round and round. Squeak. Squeak. Squeak.

And I'm back in that tiny bedroom now, walls closing in, and I turn away. I've got to get out of here. Oh yeah. I'm supposed to be looking for the bathroom. That's right. There's a dinner party downstairs. I can hear the noise again over the thumping in my head. They're laughing, not knowing that at any moment I could devour their children. The night-light's spinning stars, and I can taste the blood. I've just got to feed.

Then I see it. Stuck in a cage. A tiny little hamster, and it's drumming away on its wheel, trying to escape. Because it knows what I am, and it knows what I'll do.

Round and round and round. Squeak. Squeak. Squeak.

I leave the cage door hanging open. Maybe he got away. Maybe he's hiding in the skirting board.

Vermin's the Pot Noodle of vampire snacks. Slightly disgusted with myself, I flush what's left down the loo, and I wash my hands and I go back downstairs to the laughter and the clink of real wine. And I wish I could get that smell out of my head.

TIME FOR FUN

41

Mitchell and Denise stood outside the little pub having a cigarette. Inside, through the warped old glass, they could just see George and Annie sitting at a table, looking like they were waiting for a train.

'Good to see I'm not the only one chuffing away like a chimney,' said Denise, smiling. 'I approve.'

Mitchell looked at his cigarette and then shrugged at the people inside the bar. 'Yeah – marks Us out from Them.'

'Oh I know,' Denise said. 'We're so much more interesting cos we're dying! Ha ha.'

'Yup,' said Mitchell. 'At any moment, this could be it. The next one could be the lethal cancer stick.' He shook the packet invitingly.

'You don't believe all that, do you? Course not, you're too smart. It's like the pictures they slap on the packets, you just think it's all a bit silly. Anyway, all my fags have the warnings printed on them in Greek, so I've no sodding idea what they're saying – probably just asking politely for the return of the Elgin Marbles. Nah, It's best to just assume that you can carry on smoking and you'll be fine.'

Mitchell shrugged. 'I agree,' he said flatly. 'I genuinely think I'm immortal.'

'Uh-huh,' nodded Denise. 'You know I think you're being serious.'

Mitchell smiled, showing his teeth just slightly. 'Hello, I'm Mitchell. Have we met?'

Denise grinned and flicked her cigarette away into the night. 'So, how is Annie? How is she really?'

Mitchell was about to answer, but Denise pressed on.

'I mean, it's so odd. They were like… together almost as long as I've known them. I mean, you know like Brangelina. I mean, I'm sure they had their rows, their bust-ups, and, yeah, there was the odd time when I'd look at Owen and I'd think… but no, there was something about them. They just seemed so much more together. It's partly Annie – she's always been practical. She brought a bread-maker to college! I swear she'd have ironed Owen's t-shirts if he'd let her. Not in a little domestic slave way – but because she just liked everything to be…'

'Just so?' Mitchell laughed. 'Oh, she's still like that.'

'Yeah, but way more laid back. The old Annie would never dream of wearing those clothes to the pub.'

'Oh, she's changed all right,' said Mitchell, smiling at a private joke.

'That's what I'm worried about,' said Denise. 'But is she… You know…? OK?'

'Doing better than Owen, I bet.' Again that little smile.

'That so? How's he? I mean, I knew them both, so I guess

I'm kind of upset for him as well, a little. He was always quite a charmer, if you know what I mean. Nice guy. Always stuff to say. Snappy dresser, even at college. Do you know what he's up to now?'

Mitchell's arms reached out into the night. 'Oh, we don't see him much. Only really knew him to have the odd beer with. It's ah… perhaps Annie should… tell you the story.' He paused and smiled again. 'I'm a man. I don't talk about emotions.'

Denise smiled back, liking him just a little. 'I will – but just so long as she's OK.'

Mitchell sucked some air in through his teeth slowly. 'She's… quiet. She's living a quiet life. Doesn't go out much at the moment. Doesn't see many people.'

'Then we need to get her out of her shell!'

'You've done just that, Denise. Seriously, going to the pub is a big thing for her at the moment.'

'Really? Poor cow. We must do something. Shock treatment!'

'Er, what do you mean?' Mitchell looked briefly alarmed.

'Well,' Denise gestured inside the pub. 'About Annie. Get her up and about. I'm brilliant at it. It's my special skill as a Travel Rep. Honestly – I zero in on the quiet ones and by the end of the first week they're up on stage doing karaoke and pole dancing. That's my superpower.'

'Karaoke?' Mitchell winced. 'I genuinely fear you.'

'Quite right too,' said Denise.

Mitchell glanced nervously back into the pub. 'You know, time's a great healer.'

'And I'm better! We're going to get that woman's get-up-and-go back in the room! We are getting her her groove back, we are restoring her mojo, we are going Phil and Kirsty on her arse. Team Annie!'

'Come again?'

Denise opened the door, letting the warm air blast over them. 'Oh, well, I'm in town for a couple of weeks. And I love a project. Team Annie!' She raised her hand in a salute.

Mitchell returned it, then watched as the door banged shut behind her. 'Oh, great,' he murmured. He sniffed the air briefly, and went back inside.

Denise flopped down on the sofa and looked around. 'Where's Annie? She gone to get another round in?' she asked.

George looked up at her, immediately guilty. 'She's...' he began, and shrugged. 'Around somewhere... I'm sure.'

Denise tilted her head on one side. 'Loo?'

'Yes, ah, that'll be it.' George started to tear a beer mat into tiny pieces. 'Yup.'

Denise's hand slid over his, and he yelped. And there she was, staring at him, cleavage threatening to burst like a dam. 'I need a favour, George.'

'Oh God,' he breathed. 'Yes?'

'We're going to get Annie back up on her feet.'

'Right.'

'No, seriously. She's had a tough time and no one doesn't not have fun when I'm around,' said Denise firmly.

George tilted his head, thinking. 'I'm fairly certain you've used too many double-negatives for that to make sense. Strictly speaking.'

'George,' Denise breathed as she leaned closer. 'I don't know the meaning of the word "no".'

'I was worried you wouldn't.'

'Your catalogue boyfriend is on my side as well...' She looked up as Mitchell slid down next to her. 'Isn't that right, lover boy?' She ruffled Mitchell's hair. 'Oh he's a wild one this one, quite a devil. I bet you no girl's safe from your charms, is she? And that's how you like it, I'll swear. And that's what you're bringing to the party – you are going to charm Annie into submission. That girl's going to have more fun than she knows what to do with.'

Mitchell nodded, seriously. 'Oh, absolutely. We're going to see a whole fun side of Annie. Team Annie!' He raised a fist in the air. 'Woo,' he said, quietly.

'I see,' said George, firmly. 'And this is a good idea, is it? We have thought this through, have we?'

'I never think,' said Denise, seriously. 'There's no time for that. I just do.'

'Oh, I am pleased,' sighed George. 'And reassured. Nothing can possibly go wrong with this.'

'That's the attitude!' Denise whooped. 'Now, let's get more booze in! Where is Annie? Am I gonna have to go and fetch her out the bogs?'

'You can't!' squeaked George. 'I just remembered... she went home. She was looking a bit faint.' He stared desperately at Mitchell, who just smiled.

Denise stood up. 'Poor cow,' she said. 'But that's great – it means we can have a really good session of scheming and drinking. Come on, boys! I do all my best thinking when I'm legless and painting the town red!' Laughing, she headed off to the bar.

'Great,' muttered George. 'Because what we really need right now is to get out more.'

GOODBYE TEENS

19

'We meet again!' cried George, sliding his mop down the hospital corridor.

'*En garde!*' shouted Mitchell, running his mop into George's.

'Defend yourself, knave!' warned George, pulling back his mop and preparing to joust.

'Look to the Lady, Cardinal!' roared Mitchell, and charged.

'Oh, I love Wednesday mornings,' whispered George, ducking as the mop flicked over his head.

The battle raged along the empty corridor, the noises of the hospital fading gently away as the two twirled and thwacked their way up and down the lino, George grabbing a pin board as a shield.

'Your arm improves, whippersnapper,' chided Mitchell, leaping onto a trolley.

'I owe it all to you, Obi-Wan,' said George, executing a mock bow and a vicious jab that dislodged a ceiling tile.

The fight continued, as it normally did, until either a weary nurse confronted them or a baffled patient pottered past. That was what was great about Wednesdays – even in hospitals, nothing much seemed to happen in the early morning. That magic hour before cartloads of lukewarm toast were wheeled out to universal revulsion.

It was just two grown men, fighting like children, flicking disinfectant around and giggling. It was a highlight of George's week, a little break in the maddening tedium, but also a worrying marker point. Halfway through another week of cleaning and wheeling and putdowns and filth and honestly not thinking about Nina. Every time he'd be in a lift with a patient and would have to move out of the way, just slightly, for a doctor – and the doctor would be only a little older than him, and wouldn't even really notice him. And he'd hear his mother's voice: 'George, you should really study medicine.' Well, either that or the law or accountancy. But, oddly, never 'George, you should really learn how to clean a toilet.' Yet here he was. This had all been Mitchell's idea – he swore the best way to vanish was to be here, in this hospital, doing nothing much, earning just enough. And in a way, that was right.

But in another way it was wrong. It suited Mitchell, of course, near all that blood, keeping a watchful eye over the patients – it suited Mitchell's purposes, it suited him down to the ground. But what was there for George? At least working in that café had improved his cooking no end – he definitely wasn't River Café standard, oh no, but he was convinced he had a certain something. Admittedly he'd only professionally practised with cheap sausages and barn eggs, but even Magda had admired his corned beef omelette. He sometimes thought he should be back at that café. Yeah. He wouldn't have met Nina. It wouldn't all have gone wrong. But he'd still be there at the café... cooking away more often than not, topping up the ketchup and the brown sauce and maybe experimenting with the odd salad. Who knows? That is if he hadn't been nearly kicked to death in that alley. If Mitchell hadn't saved his life. If they hadn't got that house, if they hadn't met Annie.

So here they were, fighting with wet, soapy sticks, Mitchell pinned up against a wall, pretending to choke as George bore down on him, cursing and giggling. Passing time. *I wonder*, thought George, *what will happen to us in ten years time? I'll be looking older. But Mitchell will still be the same. And what will we be doing then? Still biding our time at a hospital.* He'd always had a funny dream about them running a second-hand bookshop, but he'd never mentioned it to Mitchell. He wasn't really sure what Mitchell read. Well, apart from *The Beano*.

Suddenly Mitchell fought back, and George was sliding across the damp floor, laughing at Mitchell stood over him, the wet end of the mop hanging inches away from his face.

'Submit!' roared Mitchell, the mop head dangling a bit closer.

'Never!' vowed George, and the mop slid a bit lower still, filthy water spilling over George's uniform.

'Submit or suffer a fate worse than death!'

And the mop dropped lower still...

'Oh, I bloody love this,' thought George to himself.

Dr Declan McGough was not loving his Wednesday. The hospital's newly appointed administrator walked along an overlit corridor, flashing grimacing greetings to the staff he passed. He took little satisfaction in observing their terrified flinches. He was, honestly, thoroughly missing London. He closed the door of his office gratefully, running a hand through his thinning hair and automatically straightening his threadbare tie. If it was up to him, he'd have liked nothing more than to be back in Whitehall, far away from the grim coalface of the National Health Service. His theoretical white papers ('Weighting Lists: A New Triage' and 'Cutting Hospital Corners') had got him some little acclaim. So much so, sadly, that when a little bit of crisis management was required, he found himself here, administrating an actual hospital. There were staffing problems, there were systems issues, and there was a surprisingly large number of mysterious deaths.

So far, nothing too awful – one scandal mostly dodged, his appointment noticed by no one, bar *Private Eye*, which had used it as an excuse to dredge up an old IT system overspend. The lazy buggers had even re-used the same bad cartoon of him – which he'd framed and hung on the wall next to an old family photo to prove that he didn't take himself too seriously. All things considered, things were going fairly well. Without too much effort, the entire staff treated him as an almost pantomime villain, which was a good thing, as the whole business of actually running a hospital was just never-ending hard work. Still the good news was that he was ready to roll out the next phase. The reason why he was really here.

McGough twisted the test tube of blood over and over in his hand and looked at the label. *Leo Willis*, it said. He thought of the effort he'd gone to to obtain it, and permitted himself a thin smile.

Placing it in his drawer, McGough crossed to his window and glared out the window at the car park. Another sour day loomed ahead. The sun sulked low in the sky, the car park was full of drab little cars, and a small collection of smokers hung around the entrance, waving round drips and cigarettes.

He scanned his emails, noticing that Janice, the hospital's head of HR was still off sick. Which was annoying, as he needed to talk to her. Do something about all that dreadful 'art' hanging on every bloody wall in the place. And perhaps find out from her who she thought was the dead wood here. From what little he'd seen of her, she was just the kind of bloodless ally he needed. But there she was, off on the sick – typical. Most disappointing. He'd have to have a few very carefully chosen words with her.

So, Dr McGough shouldered the burdens of high office alone, puttering listlessly through his emails. Staff turnover was terrible. Budgetary allocations still churning along on some kind of principle that he hadn't seen since the 1980s. Morale was pitiful. Dear Christ, their idea of fun was a bowling league. He scanned on, tutting. What he'd really like to do was get in a whole load of consultants, but some weasel would be bound to leak that to the local press.

'What a town of losers,' he sighed to himself and checked his watch.

And this morning, of course, he had a patient to see. An actual patient.

Unaware that she was being cursed, Janice Prescott woke up.

Up until a couple of days ago, she'd been the hospital's very-efficient-but-not-very-cheery HR manager. Now she was getting used to a new life of waking up in alleys, her neat little suit covered in blood.

Janice Prescott was now a vampire. It was a change in circumstances that had surprised her, but hadn't been that unwelcome. It helped, of course, that she had been on a Change Management course recently, and had flipped open her notes to the transition curve.

First had come the Let Go Space – denial, anxiety and shock – waking up screaming on a slab surrounded by men with teeth. They'd tried explaining to her, but there'd also been the anger and sadness to deal with – she had a lovely job, a nice boyfriend – things were really going well. And now this? She was suddenly supposed to be a vampire simply because some thin men in black told her so? Nuts to that.

Second had come the Frustration Zone – and Janice had realised her reactions here were typical. A feeling of helplessness, of loss and of being in limbo, and an uncertainty about a way forward. Should she work it through with her boyfriend? Or should she just go with the flow, see what happened? She was, she had to admit, somewhat distressed at the lack of a manual, a PowerPoint presentation, or even a simple handout. Nothing fancy – a few tick-boxes and bullet points would have done. She even caught herself toying with what one could be. That was before the sun had set and she experienced the sweeping hunger.

Which brought on the third and final phase – the New Horizon. Realising that she was on the up-slope of the curve, Janice leapt into being a new vampire. She'd enjoyed the killings she'd made so far, she was loving window shopping for a new look and, she had to admit, it was true what they said about a sudden change causing a drastic widening of perspective. It was all different and it was all fresh. She looked at the world through new eyes. Hungry eyes.

'Why, if it isn't everyone's favourite heartbreaker!' Denise's voice came along the corridor.

Mitchell turned around, all smiles. She was looking good, he found himself thinking. Slightly more formal. Smart jacket, with a T-shirt squeezing up an impressive display of well-tanned cleavage. She was wearing slacks, not jeans, showing off a great arse, and she was definitely wearing a nice, expensive perfume. Mitchell instantly snapped on some cheekbones.

'So this is what you do?' Denise looked at Mitchell, who was wheeling a bin full of dirty linen down to the laundry.

'Hey, it pays the bills,' he told her. 'Why, you didn't think I'd be a brain surgeon, did you?'

'Well, no, thank God,' admitted Denise. She caught her reflection in a glass door and tossed her hair from side to side. Mitchell quickly stepped to one side.

'Don't underestimate being a porter,' he said, leaning on his mop. 'We are men of hidden talents.' He winked. 'So what brings you here? Care for a demonstration of how to load an industrial washing machine?'

'No thank you.' Denise smiled. 'I had the most brilliant idea this morning. Honestly, woke up first thing and there it was! My plan to get Annie back on her feet!' She stepped a little closer, and Mitchell caught another blast of that perfume. 'It's genius. I was in the area and I just knew I had to drop in and tell you all about it. You are going to absolutely love it...'

*

George wandered down the corridor. Just another day. Long and boring. Mitchell had his iPod full of music. George had tried getting a portable radio, but Radio Four's reception was horrible, and he'd rather have nothing than spend all day listening to Coldplay. We're coming for you soon, Annie.

There was something odd about the hospital today. Some of the visitors looked a bit… odd. He sniffed the air cautiously, but didn't get much. But that old man looked… Yeah. He'd ask Mitchell about it.

Dr McGough stared at the fresh blood sample, holding it up to the light. 'Not so bad, was it?' he said.

His patient winced. 'Is it OK to look yet? I hardly dare.'

'What?' Distracted, McGough blinked. 'Yes, of course, my dear – don't worry all done. Squeamish about the sight of blood are you?'

'No, no, that's not it at all. It's just the kit you use… It's a bit grim, all those pipes and gubbins jabbing out of my arm.'

'Indeed.' McGough was warming up his bedside manner. 'Well, yes, I should imagine so. But it's wonderfully efficient.' He shook the test tube again, and placed it in a neat little cardboard container with several others.

'Now,' he said, all kindly and warm, and utterly insincere, 'here's a nice little bit of cotton wool and then I'll put a sticking plaster on for you. And we'll see you again tomorrow.'

'You're not really welcome here,' said Mitchell, tightly, blocking the vampire's path with his broom.

The young vampire shrugged. 'Go easy, boss,' he said,

his skinny shoulders shifting about uneasily in his cheap leather jacket.

'Don't call me boss,' hissed Mitchell.

'Hey!' wailed the vampire. 'It's not like we had an election. You brought down Herrick! You're like our Che Guevara, man.'

'No I'm not!' Mitchell laughed bitterly. 'I am nothing like Che Guevara. Nor Fidel Castro. You don't know who either of those people are, do you? Bet you've never even seen *Evita*.'

'Don't cry for me, Argentina,' the vampire sulked. He was dressed in emo-kid get up. Authentically. Clearly a new recruit. One of those *Twilight* fans who'd got a bit out of his depth – and suddenly it wasn't all crushed velvet and eternal love, but dark alleys and biting the heads off puking drunks.

'What are you doing in my hospital?'

'Your hospital?' The vampire smiled back. 'Your hospital now is it?'

'It is my hospital,' said Mitchell tightly. 'You're not welcome. So why are you here?'

'Dunno,' said the vampire. 'Really I don't.'

Oddly, Mitchell believed him.

'Just an urge,' the kid explained, looking around himself, a bit puzzled.

'Go on,' said Mitchell, intrigued.

'I dunno… It's just… Can you smell bacon frying?' The kid looked up at the air and sniffed.

Mitchell sniffed too and something like a smile parted his lips, showing his teeth. 'Yeah, something like that. Something like bacon.'

'I could murder a bacon sandwich,' said the kid.

'Why don't you?' asked Mitchell. 'The canteen's down the corridor. They're quite good.'

The kid shook his head. 'Nah, I'm keeping myself pure.'

Mitchell's smile faded. 'Don't be an arse. There's nothing like a bacon sandwich. Treat yourself. I promise I won't tell the rest of the undead. And then clear off.'

The kid looked at him.

Mitchell continued. 'No one can resist it, you know. It's what they use when prisoners go on hunger strike. They'll set up a little camp stove in the cell next door and they'll fry slice after slice of bacon until it goes crispy and brown. It really doesn't fail.'

The kid swallowed, and licked his lips. 'Bullshit,' he said.

Mitchell cuffed him gently round the neck. 'Go on. Have a treat. And be good.'

The kid headed off to the canteen, and, left alone once more, Mitchell leaned on his broom, and sniffed the air.

It was later that day. A lot later. George was pottering down a corridor, when something caught his eye. He had a favourite noticeboard in the hospital. It was outside Nina's ward. It was where he'd hang around most days. Even now. He'd memorised all the words on a poster about gonorrhoea. But now, something had changed. The poster had gone. It was being replaced.

'What are you doing?' asked George, crossly.

There was Mitchell, pinning something up to the board.

'It's Denise's plan,' said Mitchell, sticking the last drawing pin in. He stood back and admired his work.

'Little bit down on the left,' said George quietly. Mitchell coughed and made an adjustment, then stood back again.

'That is Denise's plan?' said George after a while.

Mitchell nodded. 'Oh yeah.'

'Does Annie know about it yet?'

'Oh no,' said Mitchell.

'I see,' said George. 'And we're going to get Annie to go along to this?'

Mitchell shook his head. 'Nope. We're getting Annie to organise it.'

George stood back and looked again at the poster. 'A Bingo night?'

Intermission
WHEN I AM OLD

Annie

When I am old? Great. Thanks for asking that. Twist the knife, why don't you? It would be me and Owen. We'd be living abroad, probably. Somewhere sunny. Maybe even Australia. We'd have a really good kitchen and a nice car. We'd have invested sensibly, I would have made sure of that, so we would have good pensions. We would go on cruises. We wouldn't be afraid to fly, because our children would live around the world.

I'm not telling you the names I came up with, but they'd have his looks. Well, the boys would. The girls definitely wouldn't get his nose. I'd worry about that at nights. Seriously. That's all I used to worry about – not that they'd get the curls, because that's good on a girl, and not that they'd inherit his murderous rage (because, you know, it didn't seem that murderous until it was), no… I just used to think that nose would look really bad on a girl. Silly isn't it?

All that planning. I'd got it all worked out. And he fitted in perfectly. My mum was just the same – as soon as Dad came along, it was like some enormous machine switched on, all the cogs and gears spinning away like a Dyson. You know, neat and efficient and very, very clean.

I was just like her. Owen and I would get a house. We'd do it up. We'd sell it on. We'd get another one. I'd make Owen practical and stable and safe. I'd decorate, he'd plumb, I'd do the curtains, he'd assemble the flat-pack. I'd even worked out that we'd get a set of pans that would see us through about ten years, and then we'd get really, really nice ones. Solid ones that are a real pain to clean and would break your foot if you dropped them, but somehow say that you've made it.

There was a plan, you see. A really good plan. And I really only got as far as the first couple of steps. I'm stuck here. In that first house. We'd not even finished decorating. My life isn't even unpacked. It's all here waiting to happen. And it never will. I'm stuck in Jail, and everyone else is passing Go, buying Mayfair and paying supertax, and taking a Chance, and winning second prize in a beauty contest. It's just like Monopoly. Only, no it isn't. It's Cluedo. It's Annie, on the stairs, with a shove.

George
What will I be like when I'm old? I don't know, I really don't. What kind of question is that, really? I've got to here. Hello mid-twenties. A few years ago, I used to think that was ever so old. Did people even really have sex after 27, I used to wonder? Not dirty old men, but normal people.

Look, I was 16: birthdays were still fun; 25 seemed such a long way away. Not such a bad time to die. After all, I am, right now, supposed to be dead, aren't I? Savaged by some animal. A few paragraphs in a paper. Parents and a girlfriend still very upset, thank you.

But no, I'm carrying on. And… well, can you imagine an old werewolf? A senile werewolf? Imagine me, a wrinkly little old man, sat nodding in the TV room of some old people's home. Maybe I've got a little stick or a zimmer thing. And there's pills and something mushy for tea and perhaps I'm nodding off, ignoring the fact that I can suddenly really smell the shit on old Mr Bavisombe and the piss on the chair… Because I've forgotten what the date is. I've forgotten that there's a full moon.

So it happens. Right there. In the TV room. Maybe no one really notices. The little old ladies carry on knitting. The men carry on watching *Coronation Street*. And I'm lying there on the floor, my bones twisting as the wolf pushes its way through… and then maybe I eat them all, tearing the room apart in a tornado of withered limbs and stinky foam cushions and pot-pourri.

But that's not likely, is it? For one thing, someone's bound to push a panic button. There's always one. And for another thing, well, there's the shock to the system. Being a werewolf is a young man's game. All that splintering and cracking – it's not a good idea when the waiting list for a hip replacement is eighteen months, is it?

So maybe that'll be it. One full moon, maybe in late middle age, I'll fall to the floor and end up like a living bearskin rug – just a doggy puddle of flesh flopping around a bit.

It's not a cheery thought is it? Sorry. But then the nice

thing is that I do not, thank God, have a pension. Looked at like that, it's OK.

Mitchell
When I am old? I'm old already. That's a stupid question. In the town I grew up in – well, 40 was old, really. Back then, everything was good for you – drinking and smoking and cutting your head off with a blunt spoon.

I mean, come on, it may not sound like the Middle Ages to you, but the 1900s was a different time. Forget about penicillin, ibuprofen, Prozac, Tamiflu. We had gin and morphine and a lot of sticky black stuff in jars that, if it wasn't actually poison, pretty much tasted like it. No vitamins, no glucosamine sulphate, no St John's Wort tablets. No five-a-day, no wheatgrass smoothies, no pomegranate juice. Back then, you just got on with living and tried not to die.

I don't know. I guess I'd have liked a wife and some kids. It's all stuff that seems such a long time ago now. A house would have been good – and kids earning enough to look after us in our old age. But… it just seems like such a fairy tale. Like the kind of things you used to draw at school – you know, a house with four windows and a door and a chimney with smoke coming out of it and green spiky grass and a wobbly fence and a blue sky with a yellow smiling sun and a little man waving at the birds? It seems as real as that.

I've seen people I've known grow old and die. And they seemed OK. Old, yeah. But OK about it. Or cross about it. Or a bit sad about it. But mostly OK about it. Not even noble. Just resigned. Mustn't grumble.

I'm wondering about me, now. I'm imagining the future. Me in a shiny foil suit on Mars. Living on Oxo cubes.

Floating to work. And still hungry. Really, really hungry.

Yeah, that's what I'll be when I'm old.

Hungry.

Denise

When I am old? Blimey, that's a big one! Dunno really. What are people supposed to say? I'd love to be one of those apple-cheeked old dears who... loves her grandchildren, who bakes a lot, who lives in a village, who doesn't wear floral print, who likes to garden.

I *will* be the kind of old woman who has a great husband with a lot of white hair and all his marbles. We will have a conservatory with a view of the garden and the sea and we will both sit in there and laugh while drinking coffee (probably decaf at our age).

I will have several children – I will get on very well with two of them, not so well with the other one, but secretly we will have the most fun together at weddings.

When I reach 70, I will take up smoking again, and maybe learn to ride a bike or scuba-dive or hang-glide.

Because I will be the kind of old woman who has lived so long that I won't be afraid to take risks.

CLICKETY-CLICK

66

'Bingo night?' Annie was incredulous.

George looked around the kitchen, frightened that stuff was going to start flying around. Which would take a lot of explaining.

Mitchell just smiled at him. *It'll be fine.*

'Oh yeah, it'll be an utter laugh, you'll love it, Annie darling,' said Denise, grinning, and passing over a flyer. 'It'll be great. Trust me.'

'I. Don't. Even. Know. How. To. Play. Bingo. I'm not an old lady,' sighed Annie.

'Listen to Miss Sudoku.' Denise rolled her eyes, draining the stiff gin and tonic George had made her. 'Bingo is so now! Seriously – used to do it all the time with my holidaymakers. Right laugh. Of course, we played it with whipped cream, but this is going to be Old School. And it's going to be amazing.'

Annie looked at the flyer again, not trusting herself to pick it up.

'I didn't even know there was a local sports centre.'

'It's more of a hut, really.' said George. 'You know that playing field down the hill?'

'What?' laughed Annie. 'With the shed?'

'Yup,' said Mitchell. 'That's the sports centre.'

'Right,' said Annie.

'As I said, this is all in a good cause.' Denise pushed merrily along. This was, George just knew, the voice she used when flogging sightseeing trips on inflatable bananas. 'They want to do the place up. There are two lovely little old dears who've been running these Bingo nights, and they've not been going well. Poor loves. They need a secret weapon – you and me and a whole bag of fun. So I dropped in on them and offered our expertise. They jumped at the chance. And quite right too.'

'Our expertise?' Annie laughed.

'Our expertise.' Denise was firm. 'I know all about Bingo and you know how to put together a great party.' Annie opened her mouth, but Denise sailed on. 'Of course you do, luv. She did this great thing for someone's 21st – decorated their whole flat. Kind of a James Bond theme. Amazing. Took days it did. And then, on the big night, she and Owen spent the whole time shagging in the spare room.'

Annie coughed. 'We did not.'

George and Mitchell started to examine different patches of wallpaper.

'Did too,' said Denise. 'You were on the coats. I had to walk home in a bikini. It was raining.'

'Anyway,' said George.

'Yeah,' said Mitchell. 'The point is Annie can throw a

good party. It's a great chance. You can get out… SEE new people. Get on like a house on fire.'

'Maybe meet the next Owen,' put in Denise.

'I bloody hope not,' said Annie.

Inevitably, Denise dragged them out for drinks. George muttered that it was a school night, but even Annie seemed in the mood.

Just for a quick one.

As Mitchell turned to lock the door, George looked around. 'Did you see that?'

'What?' asked Mitchell, suddenly alert and sniffing the air.

'I'm sure I saw…' Then George noticed Denise looking at him, puzzled. 'Er…'

'There's a gang at the bottom of the road,' said Annie, brightly. 'They're a bit… you know.'

'Gothic,' said Mitchell, his smile not reaching his eyes. 'Emo kids.'

Denise rolled her eyes. 'An emo gang? What do they do? Sulk you into giving them your wallet?'

'Oh no,' said Annie. 'They're pretty bloodthirsty. The little, um, buggers.'

'I hate it whenever those weird little emo kids turn up at the resort. You can't do anything with them. They don't want to get a tan, they don't want to go swimming, they don't want to go on any trips, they just slouch around re-reading their *Twilight* books and complaining about the lack of wi-fi. I always wonder why they bother going on holiday. Can't the police do anything about them hanging around on your road?'

'Ah,' said Mitchell, 'Let's just say the police are involved.

I'm sure it's sorting itself out.'

'Yeah,' said George, unconvinced. 'But what are they doing hanging out in the street at this time of day…? In our street?'

Mitchell clapped a hand on his friend's shoulder. 'Come on, George, let's not worry about it too much. Not when there's pub. We don't want Denise thinking it's not safe to walk the streets at night.'

'But it's *not* safe to walk the streets at night,' whispered George.

Denise laughed. 'Oh, I can look after myself, believe me,' she said.

So off they went to the pub, George trying not to glance around fearfully. Something felt wrong in the air.

George's unease continued at the pub. Denise was on good form, and laughing and laughing, and he noticed that Mitchell had sat close to her. Did he fancy her, he wondered? Did she fancy him? Nearly all girls did.

Just once, he thought, it'd be nice to meet an unsexy vampire. Even Herrick had copped off with that dinner lady. It's like they had some kind of built-in sex appeal.

Not that, ah, he hadn't. Really. It was just he was a bit different about these things.

He looked at Denise and tried to work out if he found her attractive, but there was just a weird… no. Not really. Like maybe he did, but there was something about her…

Then he looked at Annie, trying to toy with her drink, trying not to be obvious about the fact that she was feeling really nervous. It was almost like when they'd first met her. She just seemed… less there, somehow. Less linked to the world.

And that wasn't helping. George wondered if it was something to do with his wolf senses. But everything felt odd tonight. Like his fur was tingling. Like he had a nasty school maths test the next day, or an exam or something. Like he was in trouble. Like something really terrible was about to happen.

He looked around the bar, trying to tune into conversations, trying not to stare at people. Somehow, something told him… no. Something *was* wrong.

The problem was, not all the vampires looked like vampires. There were a few who dressed all in black. So what about in this pub? It was a bit busy, there were quiet Sunday evening couples, a few friends sharing out wine and crisps, nothing extraordinary.

He noticed the toilet door bang shut, a flash of dark hair.

'Hmm,' he said. 'Excuse me, I'll just go to the little boys' room,' and left them, noticing Denise rolling her eyes.

CLEAN THE FLOOR

54

As the door swung closed behind George, the sounds of the pub swept away, replaced by dim lighting, the gush of a cistermiser and the smell of ammonia and kidney infections. The two men were stood at the urinal, and George suddenly realised that this was a peculiar situation.

Why hadn't he brought Mitchell with him? Mitchell would just breeze in here, say something witty, flush their heads down the nearest toilet and take control of the situation.

But George was not Mitchell. And he had no idea what to do. He stared at the men's backs. They didn't seem particularly vampiric. One of them turned around and glanced at him and George realised nervously he was just standing there. He coughed and smiled a little and then went to the sink and started to wash his hands. Carefully, of course. That was the thing about working in a hospital.

It had taught him really good hand hygiene. It was why, he thought, he hadn't got swine flu. It's so easy really. Lots of soap, water not too hot (why do they always make the hot water so hot in bathrooms?), backs of the hands, front of the hands, and scrub and rinse and... George was happily absorbed for a few seconds in washing his hands, and trying to angle himself so that he could see the men in the mirror. That'd tell him. But no. So he risked another glance, all casual, over his shoulder. Both were still at the urinal. Still not very vampiric.

George stuck his hand under the dryer, but it was broken.

So, with a lack of anything else to do, he stood next to them at the urinal.

He realised two things. First of all, there was absolutely, definitely, certainly no way he was going to be able to pee. No chance of that at all. Secondly, unless he'd just been delivering baby lambs, what man washes his hands before taking a leak? He was now certifiably odd...

He was also standing next to two suspected vampires at a urinal. He looked dead ahead of him, and willed the stream. The poster on the wall was about STDs, and featured a pair of jeans with the slogan *You don't know what's in their pants*.

'Like that's helping,' he said.

He realised he'd spoken out loud.

'Sorry,' he said, turning to them both with a watery smile, 'It's just... Why do they advertise STDs in here? It's not like I'm suddenly going to look down and notice a pus-like discharge,' he babbled on. 'Or that I'm going to say to you, "Excuse me, but I couldn't help noticing the genital warts on your –" Ah... I mean, that's not going to happen is it? I mean, for one thing, who speaks to people in the Gents?'

The men continued to stare at George. George stared back.

'Um,' said George. 'Uncomfortable. Sorry. But I have to ask. I mean, I'm actually having quite a nice quiet night out and I couldn't help noticing the two of you. And I was wondering... ah...'

The men stared at George, and one of them grinned.

'Look... it's not that I think you're gay. Not that there's anything wrong with that, no, no. It's just...'

The men looked at George.

'And I know how this seems, and I am so sorry if I've got this wrong, but is there the tiniest chance that you're vampires?'

Denise laughed, setting down more drinks. 'I've got you another one, Annie. Even though you're nursing that one a bit.'

Annie shook her head, resting a hand, just about, over her glass. 'Oh, I've really cut down. You know how it is. Don't want to become that kind of ex-girlfriend. Two pinot grigios and a river of self-pity.'

'Tell me about it!' Denise settled down on the sofa, a fraction closer to Mitchell than she had been before, Annie noticed. 'You can spot them almost before they get off the resort bus. The Suddenly Single Sandras only just holding back the tears. It just needs one wheel to go on their wheelie luggage and boom! Total meltdown. They're such easy prey for waiters at the resort. Officially, I'm supposed to stop that kind of thing, but it's the best thing for them, poor loves. Just what they need. Honestly, there's this one guy, Panos... Oh My God. He deserves an award from UNESCO. Some of them can barely sit down for the bus ride back to the airport, but they're grinning from ear to ear. I bet you're like that, aren't you, Mitchell?' and she jabbed him in the ribs. 'Patients hurling themselves at you?'

Mitchell turned to her, a catlike grin on his face, 'Not so much, no,' he said. 'Hospitals really aren't randy places. Well, except on the Alzheimer's ward.'

'Oh,' said Denise, and sipped at her drink. 'Well, I'm sure there's a fair few nurses who've got a good word to say about you.'

'Not really,' said Mitchell, tightly. His grin faded slightly.

Annie covered over the awkward moment. 'Where's George?' she asked. 'He's been a while.'

Mitchell tossed a peanut in the air. 'He's always had a shy stream, if you know what I mean. He's probably coaxing as we speak.'

Denise smirked. 'Aww. He's a sweet boy. Bet he's got a big one though.' She cackled. 'It's always the same with the nervous ones. Whereas I bet Mitchell here is hung like a snail. Don't you think, Annie?'

'Uh,' said Annie.

'Oh come on, you can't live with two blokes and not know this kind of thing. Surely you've caught a sneaky peek while they're showering? First thing I'd do.'

'You haven't, have you?' asked Mitchell, alarmed. 'I mean, Annie's quite quiet when she wants to be. Quiet as a ghost.'

'Mitchell!' gasped Annie.

'Oh, is she now?' said Denise, suddenly sharp.

George stood there, the men facing him.

'Hello,' said George, trying a jaunty wave.

'Hi,' said one of the men. He was taller and had a lot of stubble.

'So,' said George, 'I'm right aren't I? Which is, oddly, a relief. I mean, I'm so glad you're not gay. That would have been so embarrassing.' He rolled his eyes and tried for a hearty laugh.

'But you're fine that we're vampires?' asked the other man slowly. He swept his blond hair off his face and stared at George, disbelieving.

'Oh yes,' said George, drawing himself up slightly. 'I am totally at home with the vampires. I know exactly how to deal with you.'

The first vampire coughed, slightly. 'Your flies are undone,' he said.

'Oh,' said George, and looked down.

And then they were on him.

Mitchell up-ended the packet and tipped the last of the peanuts into his mouth, before dabbing at the remains.

Denise shuddered. 'Go easy on them nuts, Mitchell,' she said. 'The sodium in that one bag alone…'

'Oh,' said Mitchell, 'I need a lot of salt in my diet.'

It was the wrong time of the month. The wolf part of George had very little to offer in the fight. Except a smell, a smell that annoyed vampires.

He struggled, but the blond one held his arms behind his back while the other one hit him in the stomach.

Mitchell and Denise were laughing. Laughing about something. Annie experimented and just about managed to run her finger round the rim of her wine glass. That was something, she supposed. She let her eyes wander across the pub, wondering sadly why she hadn't picked this one to work in. It looked nice. It was quite busy. No psychos.

Nice and busy. Happy people having a happy little drink. Busy being alive. Denise working her magnetic charm on Mitchell. Mitchell happy to be charmed. And suddenly Annie alone. The loneliest person in the whole world.

Her eyes settled for a second too long on the horse racing on the television. 'And coming up, it's Fearful Vengeance,' cried the announcer. 'Followed by Men With Sticks and Eternal Suffering in the lead, and, as they come into the last straight it's Oh, Annie We're Coming To Get You trailing behind… and yes, with Eternal Suffering first past the post, Oh Annie is definitely the loser.'

She looked quickly away, clapping her hands over her ears. Her eyes wandered to a slot machine. The fruit machine dials spun round and round and came up with three nooses.

And on the Deal Or No Deal quiz-o-matic, she could see Noel Edmonds, eyes burning with the fires of hell, getting ready to offer her a really bad deal from the Banker.

The cacophony built, and all she could see was Denise and Mitchell. Laughing and happy. And… something was wrong, wasn't it?

George coughed up a bit of blood.

The vampire leaned over him. 'Pity it's dog,' he sighed. 'What a waste. I'd rather drink piss.' He hit him again, and George cried out.

The vampire laughed. 'And your odour! That stench is almost blocking out the… the smell. The reason we came here. Maybe once we've finished with you, the reek will stop, and everything will smell all right again. What do you think, doggie?'

A blow landed on his jaw.

George tried to ignore the pain. He wondered how long he would have to wait until either he passed out or until somebody, surely, would need to use the loo. *I mean, this is a pub full of men. At least twenty of them, nearly all of them drinking pints. And at least some of them must have broken the seal by now, which means that let's say that's ten men needing to pee every half hour, that's a ratio of one every six minutes, mind you, minus three for us. Now, that would mean maybe about one every nine minutes. I wonder how long they've been hitting me for?*

He struggled and tried to fight back, tried to concentrate on the sums, but he could just feel the pain getting worse. And, riding over it, the memory of lying in that gutter outside the café, and the beating and the pain and wishing it would just stop.

Then he saw her in the mirror.

'Oh hi,' said Mitchell. He'd been staring at Denise's eyes and now looked at Annie. 'Thought you'd gone.'

'I went to The Toilet,' she said heavily.

'Good for you.' Mitchell was slurring his voice slightly.

'Didn't see you go,' said Denise. 'You weren't long.'

'No, I wasn't. Not as long as George has been,' said Annie, meaningfully. 'Perhaps he's In Trouble. Really Bad Trouble.'

Mitchell shrugged. 'Nah, just doing a Number Two.'

'In a public toilet?' said Annie. 'This is George. And it's not 8.20 a.m.'

'Good point,' said Mitchell, standing up a little woozily.

59

'I'll go and see if he's all right. He's probably run out of paper.' He stumbled off to the loo.

Denise turned to Annie. 'God, he's hammered on two beers? You didn't tell me you lived with a couple of lightweight milk drinkers.'

Annie, her mind elsewhere, her eyes fixed on the toilet door, just shrugged.

Denise sat up suddenly. 'Oh God, Annie,' she gasped. 'There's something you're not telling me about them. I just knew it!'

Annie, guiltily, spun round, managing not to sink into the sofa. 'Um...'

Denise clapped her hands. 'Oh no!' she shrieked, 'They're Christians!'

Mitchell swung open the toilet door and stared at the devastation, at George, punch drunk and slumped in the blond vampire's grip. He folded his hands.

'Evening lads,' he breezed.

The vampires looked at him. 'We are house training the dog,' said one.

'I think you can stop that,' Mitchell told him.

'He's been a bad boy and we're going to rub his nose in it.'

'No, no you're not.' said Mitchell, calmly. 'You see, it's a nice night, I'm a bit drunk, you're a lot drunk and we all make mistakes, especially when we're plastered. So I'm going to be absolutely open with you. Either you put him down and leave, or I very slowly rip your heads off.' And his eyes went dark.

'Well,' said Annie. 'Not so much Christian. You see, Mitchell had a rigorous Catholic upbringing. He's just come out of a seminary, in fact.'

'A defrocked priest!' gasped Denise. 'So I've been barking up the wrong tree? Typical Denise! Excuse me for having pubic hair and the wrong genitals.'

'No,' sighed Annie. 'Not like that. Just a lack of faith. He just couldn't carry on doing what he was supposed to do. So now he's not. Kind of extreme denial.'

'Oh,' gasped Denise. 'Oh that's so brave. The poor lamb.'

'And that's why the... poor lamb's working in a hospital,' Annie continued, babbling slightly, 'You know, doing good works in the community.'

'And George?'

'Jewish,' said Annie firmly. 'Very very Jewish. That's why he seems so... fussy. Compulsive. It's a lifetime of not touching light switches on a Friday.'

'Oh,' said Denise. 'And these are your stabiliser wheels?' She shrugged. 'Well, I guess after Owen... I mean, he was your typical bad boy.'

'Tell me about it,' sighed Annie, glancing again at the toilet door.

'So come on,' said Denise. 'Which of them do you fancy? I mean, surely you must fancy one of them?'

'Thank you,' said George, leaning over the sink while Mitchell dabbed him down with wet toilet paper.

'Yeah,' said Mitchell. 'We're lucky they just left. I've not... really got it in me to fight them off tonight. Don't know what it is. Bit drunk to tell you the truth.'

'You?' George winced as he dabbed himself down gently.

'Yeah,' said Mitchell. 'Dunno. But hey, let's try and get you in some state.'

'I thought there was a truce.'

'Yes.' Mitchell had dropped a blood-soaked wad in the sink and was now looking at his lack of a reflection in the mirror. 'Yes there is. But something's up.'

'The *smell*, they said,' George muttered. 'Apparently. Mean anything to you?'

Mitchell shrugged and waited for his lack of a reflection to do the same. 'Nope, means nothing to me. Maybe they were just drunk and fancied a bit of action.'

George straightened up, and the hand-dryer whirred into action, blowing a dribble of blood across his face. 'Oh now you work,' he snapped. 'Thank you very much.'

Annie and Denise were laughing when George and Mitchell came back.

'No? Him? Really?' gasped Denise. They both stopped and looked guilty.

'Nosebleed,' moaned George weakly, dabbing at his nose with a tissue.

'Oh,' said Denise. 'Tilt your head back and drink a glass of water.'

'That,' said George with dignity, 'is the cure for hiccups.'

'I know,' said Denise. 'I just wanted to see if you'd try it.'

George pulled a face.

'One more drink?' asked Denise, and headed off to the bar. 'Make you feel better.'

'Your friend is an alcoholic,' complained George, nervously watching her at the bar.

'She's just fun.' Annie was defensive. 'Although, watching her knock them back, I could absolutely murder a pint. I haven't got off my face for two years. It's like I'm on the worst diet in the world, and I'm not losing weight. How stupid is that?'

Mitchell finished his drink and made an equivocal dip with his fingers. 'Booze takes the edge off immortality. Trust me.'

'Great,' sighed Annie. 'No wonder ghosts run up and down stately homes screaming at people. Anything for a laugh.' She turned to George. 'Now that she's gone – are you all right?'

'Battered,' whimpered George. 'It was the wrong time to fight two vampires.'

'You brave thing,' tutted Annie. 'But what were they doing here? Not exactly rich pickings for vampires, is it?'

Mitchell shrugged. 'George, you should have told me. I'd have sent them packing straight away. No real harm in them.'

'No real harm?' George roared, his voice coming out an octave too high. He coughed. 'No real harm? They tried to take out my teeth with a urinal.'

'Ah well, high spirits,' said Mitchell. 'I'm off for a fag.' He shuffled away.

'Is he all right?' asked Annie.

George watched him go. 'I don't know. He seems... drunk.'

Annie nodded. His attempt to impress Denise was trying a bit too hard. 'That's typical Denise behaviour. Men try and keep up with her. It doesn't always go so well. Her liver must be made out of ceramic. I remember having to hold Owen's head over a bucket once.'

'She sounds exhausting,' said George, looking at her meaningfully.

Annie clocked the look and smiled. 'No, it's fine. It's great having her around. She's fun. Come on. Shake things up a bit. It's what we all need.'

'Is it?' said George, uncertainly. 'I just mean... I'm sure she's great fun and all that, and that's very nice. It's just that I'm not sure it's really... what we need.'

Mitchell stood outside, smoking. He was starting to sober up a little, he noticed. Cool night air. He shook his head, exhaling smoke like a woozy dragon. And he grinned. He was in the mood for a good fight.

He looked out at the street. Something moved at the end of it. Keeping to the shadows. He blinked, trying again to focus. A couple of old figures, shuffling.

Betty and Arnold, the pensioner vampires. A couple who'd been in their eighties since the Sixties. Shuffling past in their tatty cardigans. Betty trailing an ancient shopping bag on wheels behind her. They noticed that Mitchell was looking at them and smiled uneasily.

'Good evening, Mitchell dear,' said Betty.

Mitchell nodded back. 'Can I help you?' he called.

Arnold looked up, his red-ringed eyes flickering a vague black. 'No, no, no, lad. Don't want to trouble you. The missus and I...' He trailed off.

'Bit of night air, dearie.'

'Yes. Lovely evening, isn't it? Smells nice.'

Mitchell nodded, uncertainly.

Betty cut in again, tapping her shopping bag. 'I've got some lovely vermin in here – rats, fox and a stray cat. Just let me know if you want anything, won't you? We hear you're very powerful these days.'

The sides of the bag, Mitchell noticed, were moving and

a low whimpering was coming from it.

He shook his head. 'I'm just keeping out of trouble. Like you two.'

'Oh that's right,' cooed Betty. 'Anything for a quiet life, that's us.'

Mitchell finished his cigarette and put it in the bin.

Betty drew her squeaking trolley closer and tutted. 'You want to give that up, dear. Sets a bad example to the youngsters.'

Mitchell shrugged. 'There's no harm in it. Like we can get cancer.'

'But it looks wrong, dear. Everyone's giving up. Soon it'll only be vampires.'

Arnold's quavering voice struck out across the night. 'I gave up in 1975. I do miss it.'

'Well, I'll take it on board,' said Mitchell soothingly.

The three of them stood awkwardly on the road, Arnold's attention wandering, Betty looking nervously around, as though hunting for something.

'Is there anything I can help you with?' asked Mitchell again.

Arnold shook his head and muttered something.

'Oh no, dear,' said Betty firmly. 'We're just out taking the midnight air. It's so pleasant tonight, isn't it?'

She sniffed the air and smiled.

'Probably just the smell of that cigarette,' said Arnold wistfully.

'No, dear. It's like Night Scented Stock, or Mint,' said Betty. 'Lovely air.'

'Yeah,' agreed Mitchell, and watched them shuffle and squeak away into the darkness.

*

'Phew!' Denise exclaimed, banging the drinks down on the table. 'Took so long to get served, I figured, let's push the boat out, so I got shooters too! Let's get rat-arsed and go clubbing!'

George looked at Annie. Annie looked at George, helplessly.

'She is trying to kill us,' whispered George.

MEN WITH ROPE AND STICKS

26

George and Mitchell sat in the canteen, not looking at each other.

'Everything hurts,' groaned George, cradling his head in his hands.

'That woman,' sighed Mitchell. 'I am sweating vodka,'

George reached out for his egg sandwich, lifted back the edge of it, then dropped it with a sour face, 'I can't even face that.'

Mitchell opened an eye carefully and winced. 'I haven't been dancing like that since the 1980s. That woman,' he said again, forcefully. 'I bet even Annie's hung over.'

'I wish she was,' said George.

'George! What's that supposed to mean?'

'I thought Denise would notice Annie wasn't drinking anything. So I...'

'George?' Mitchell prompted. 'What have you done?'

'I finished all her drinks for her when Denise wasn't looking,' said George miserably.

Mitchell laughed. 'Quite a night, eh?'

'All right for some,' muttered George, sourly. He flooded his sandwich with an ocean of ketchup and started chewing at it experimentally.

Mitchell punched him fondly on the shoulder. 'And you really went for it on the dance floor, my man.'

'Did I?' winced George. 'I don't think I can feel my legs and I'm fairly sure a rib's cracked.'

'Well, you shouldn't have gone breakdancing so soon after getting beaten up.'

'Breakdan…?' George dropped his sandwich and looked sharply at Mitchell. 'Har har.'

'No seriously,' said Mitchell. 'It was quite a night. That woman – she makes me feel my age. All those drinks, and dancing… and those vampires.'

'Yes,' said George, carefully nibbling at his sandwich. 'There were quite a few around last night, weren't there?'

Mitchell nodded. 'We could have taken them on. If we'd wanted to. Even three sheets to the wind. Mind you, they just seemed to want to dance. And there's nothing wrong with that, you know.'

'Don't you think it's a little odd? Vampires are going out clubbing together… Whatever happened to sulking in corners? Some of them were doing "Come on Eileen".'

Mitchell frowned. 'Please, not today. No new concepts.'

'It's just everywhere we go, recently, there are vampires. Are they up to something?' Sandwich finished, George started to lick the ketchup off his fingers. Mitchell shuddered.

'Don't make me think, eh, George? In a few minutes'

time I've got to go collect sheets from Ward D. I need a clear head for that.'

'They're stalking you, that's what it is. I'm sure there were even some skulking around Jason Doner Van when we got kebabs.'

Mitchell winced. 'Shut up and leave me alone.'

'OK,' murmured George, reaching across the table 'Do you want this sandwich?'

Mitchell shook his head. 'I might die.'

'That was quite a night, really,' said Annie to the teddy bear.

Annie was tidying Mitchell's room and talking to the teddy bear. She often did it during the day, some time after *The Jeremy Kyle Show* and before *Hollyoaks*. George's room didn't really need tidying. And the one time she'd done it anyway, he'd called her in and explained the ordering system for his socks to her and she'd gone away.

Mitchell's room, though, was like a perpetual teenager's, the sheets always left tangled, T-shirts and wrist bands and bits of army surplus weaved around empty glasses and stained paperbacks and CDs freed from their cases and the odd cigarette stub. Every day Annie would go up there and tidy away the mess, restoring order. And Mitchell never said thanks. Well, he had once remarked about how nice it was having a poltergeist who tidied things up, but that was it.

But it did, in truth, give her something to do. That was the problem with being a ghost. It was boring. Not much variety, really. All the normal points of life were gone – no sleep, no meals, no drink. No getting drunk. She just *was*. And, if she decided not to be, then it wouldn't be like sleep.

It'd be more like turning the television to standby. She'd just fade away for a bit – neither there or not there.

Annie had never really been a morning person. Oh, she'd usually been up before Owen, making tea (for her) and coffee (for him), and dallying with some breakfast idea or other – perhaps porridge or smoothies or grapefruit segments in a chilled metal bowl. Mostly just watching him eat. She'd be standing there, yawning into her dressing gown, soullessly spooning out the bits of grapefruit, blinking her eyes open as she stirred the porridge round and round and just dying for another bit of sleep.

Now she had all the sleep she could ever want. Only it wasn't really sleep. Not at all. She never felt tired. She never felt awake. She just felt a bit Monday. For Annie there was no such thing as a weekend lie-in, there was no mid-morning break with a cup of posh coffee, there wasn't even the guilty joy of grabbing a filthy lunch of a packet of Ready Salted and a Snickers. There was just time spent in the house.

That was what she'd loved about the pub, about the feeling it gave her of being able to go somewhere, of being able to pass time with other people. People who were busy enough not to notice that she didn't drink herself, and that occasionally, just occasionally, her feet didn't quite touch the ground.

But now she was back in the house. And, truth be told, she'd been avoiding Jeremy Kyle ever since he'd started telling her about the vengeance of Hell, and now even *Hollyoaks* was off the menu – ever since the McQueen sisters had started wearing hoods and carrying flails, and spending their time roasting alive patrons of the Dog In The Pond. She'd tuned into a re-run of *Friends*, but when she'd seen everyone sitting on a burning sofa, flames pouring out of their charred skulls, she'd switched off and given up on television.

Which left books. The problem with George and Mitchell was that they were men. And, no matter how you explained it to them, they couldn't be relied upon to bring home the latest *Heat*, or even a semi-regular bit of *Take A Break*. Funnily enough, Mitchell never forgot *The Beano*, which was kind of sweet, but not the point.

She'd been thrilled when they'd first moved in, as the bookshelves had been a bit random. She'd always loved books when she was young, and loved it when Owen had put up all the shelves. They'd talked about how they were going to arrange things – his books on one shelf, hers on another… and then they'd decided, no, let's just put all our books together. And that had been a brilliant afternoon, arranging all of them, in careful order. She had all the Narnia books, he had all of *Lord of the Rings*. They'd had two copies of *The Beach*, so one had gone to charity, but other than that it had looked brilliant.

Then, when she'd first been dead, she'd read a lot. Walking round that empty house, reading all the books she'd bought and honestly meant to get around to reading. Those old Christmas presents about the history of spices, the cookery books, even *101 Things To Do Before You Die*. She realised, sadly, she'd managed only a couple of dozen.

Until, one day, she'd been aware that the house was emptied, most of the furniture moved, and all the books gone. Nothing to do. And then, as people moved in and moved rapidly out, a few books had arrived, the odd newspaper, piling up in corners and left behind on shelves. Mostly disappointing, but she'd read them anyway, like a days-old newspaper on a foreign holiday, devouring sports reports and country diaries and Sven Hassell.

Now she was reading again. Mitchell's old comics, George's tattered paperbacks. She'd been to Hogwarts and Manderley again, she'd had a crack at Jane Austen, and noticed that Mitchell had marked some significant passages in *The Da Vinci Code* and wondered.

Recently, though, that too had stopped being as comforting as she'd hoped. She'd been ploughing through an old Dickens that George was using to prop up his chest of drawers and suddenly:

'A Merry Christmas to us all, my dears! God bless us!'

Which all the Cratchit family re-echoed.

'God bless us every one!' said Tiny Tim, the last of all. 'Even Annie.'

And Mrs Cratchit wiped her rosy-red forehead with the steaming cloth and let out a brave sigh. 'Poor dear,' she cried with zeal. 'Never was a goose so cooked as hers!'

'Hurrah!' cried the two young Cratchits. 'Hurrah!'

'Spirit!' said Scrooge, with an interest he had never felt before, 'tell me if Tiny Tim will live.'

'Oh, he'll be fine by page seventy-six,' said the Ghost. 'But spare a thought for Annie, who, if these shadows remain unaltered by the Future, will be most likely to suffer an eternity of torment, unless she be like to pass on sharpish, and so decrease the surplus population.'

'Well, spirit,' said Scrooge heartily, 'that's what I'd do if I were in her unhappy shoes.'

Annie had clapped the book shut and just sat there on the floor by the fireplace. Then she'd got up and got on with the cleaning.

Something very strange was happening, that she knew. She didn't know how long things could keep happening, and she had an urge to tell Denise. Denise would know. She'd understand. She'd even be able to help her.

But Denise seemed…

'Oh teddy,' said Annie, settling down on Mitchell's neatened duvet cover. 'She just seems a bit different. She's like Denise used to be, but, it's not just that she's older. She's sadder, somehow.'

Annie remembered the previous night, in that little club. It had been a Wednesday night in the centre of town. It hadn't been that remarkable, really. The club had been fairly quiet when they'd got there, heading down some steps, under a bridge, and into a strange little dip at the bottom of a hill. The club itself looked like a bit of an old shack, or a burnt-out off licence. The walls were painted red, the glitter balls were sparkling and the music was too loud. The barmen had ignored them all and Denise had started dancing on an empty floor.

Then it had got busy. Annie couldn't remember how. She knew she hadn't got drunk, but somehow time had just flown past. George and Mitchell had seemed really hammered all of a sudden, nearly winning the karaoke competition with a duet. And the crowd had applauded, and had all been… what had been wrong with the crowd? Annie tried to remember.

'What was it, teddy?' she asked, but the bear had no response. Annie just remembered feeling alone and left out. There was Denise, dancing, in her element. There were the two men in Annie's life staggering around and laughing helplessly. And there was she. Standing at the bar without even a chance of catching anyone's attention. There's Denise, just stomping back into her life and stealing it.

'Yeah, that's it,' said Annie, gripping the teddy's ears

perhaps a little tightly. 'She just wants to steal my life. Swan in, make everything all HD, and then bugger off back to Greece. Maybe she'll invite them on holiday. Which'll be just great. Not like I can go on holiday. Or even get a tan.' She sighed. No, that still wasn't it. Somewhere, at the back of her head, something itched.

And then later that night, as they'd all stood leaning up against the kebab van and Annie had waved away wanting anything, Denise had seemed in her element. The boys were really drunk, so drunk Annie had worried about what taxi would take them. But Mitchell couldn't stop laughing, and George was giggling, and they sat down on the steps of the museum and ate doner kebabs, and Annie again caught something in Denise's eye... like she was only pretending to be drunk.

Annie's eye had wandered to the people wandering up and down the street past them. There was something about them all... something odd...

Then Mitchell had laughed. 'Isn't this the best kebab ever?' he'd said. 'It just tastes brilliant.'

'That will be the chilli sauce,' said George, solemnly, a lopsided grin on his face. 'It never fails. I wish they sold that stuff for the home.'

'Trust me, no, you don't.' Mitchell shook his head. 'I've had a great evening. Haven't you had a great evening, Annie?'

Annie had nodded, watching the people go up and down the hill; more people, surely, than she was used to? What had all these people been doing out at night? Where had they come from? Where were they going to?

And Denise had laughed again, and put down her jacket potato almost uneaten. 'Come on, guys, let's go on somewhere!' she'd said.

The boys had giggled, And the three of them had run off to find a taxi, leaving Annie stood behind.

'Is that what it's going to be like?' muttered Annie, hugging the bear. 'A boring ghost, cleaning an empty house talking to someone else's stuffed toy?'

The doorbell rang. Annie replaced the teddy bear on the bed and went to answer it.

She always left the teddy bear on the bed. And whenever she looked in, Mitchell had always hidden it at the back of a cupboard.

Annie opened the door and there was Denise, sunglasses on, smiling tightly.

'Hey, doll,' she said. 'How's your day? Not got work?'

'Oh, just cleaning,' said Annie, inviting her in. 'You know, just catching up with stuff.'

Denise came in and sat down, plonking a paper cup of expensive coffee on the table. Annie caught a whiff of cinnamon and hot milk.

Denise sighed. 'I'm rough as Jordan.'

'Oh me too,' said Annie eagerly. 'I am very, very hung over.' She hoped she didn't sound too wistful.

'Really?' said Denise, lowering her sunglasses slightly. 'Only you barely touched a drop.'

'Tell me about it,' said Annie quickly. 'As I said, I'm a total lightweight these days.'

'I can't pack them away like I used to, either,' said Denise. 'Still – last night was wild. I'm sure I'm getting a bit old for it all.'

'Aren't we all?' said Annie.

'Well,' laughed Denise, 'you only live once, eh?'

'What brings you round so early? The boys have gone to work. What little you left of them.'

'Oh I know, they're such pussies,' said Denise. 'You'd think they'd never gone out on the lash.'

'You made them do karaoke. George… and Mitchell…'

'Oh, those boys! They need to get out and see the world a bit,' said Denise, confirming Annie's worst fears. 'Karaoke's good for the soul.' She seemed serious. 'Now come on, you. Put down that duster and let's go meet the girls. We've got a lot of Bingo work to do.'

Annie thought about protesting, but couldn't see much of a point. Instead they headed out for Bingo.

Two Fat Ladies

88

The sports hall wasn't somewhere Annie had ever really noticed before. It was down the hill, past the shops and off the edge of the park on a scrubby little bit of land covered with balding grass. Two forlorn goals hung with tattered orange string.

She noticed two figures watching them, both thin and haggard. They could have been walking their dogs, only they had no dogs. They were standing just beyond the touchline, watching them.

Annie shivered. 'You expect to see vultures overhead.'

'Frankenstein's Scout Hut,' Denise laughed. 'We'll soon cheer this place up.'

'With Bingo?' Annie said.

Denise knocked on the pitch-pine door to the hut. 'You would be surprised. Get ready for Aladdin's cave.'

The door swung open, and two remarkable old ladies

were revealed peering cautiously out into the daylight.

'Rainbow and Moonpaw!' beamed Denise. 'Hello! How you girls doing?'

'Pensioner hippies!' Annie gasped. Rainbow and Moonpaw were two glorious remnants of the Sixties. Rainbow was wearing several headscarves and a lime fleece shoved over a shawl and an ancient Laura Ashley floral-print dress. She looked at Denise. 'Oh hello, dear,' she wheezed with a voice that seemed to be leaking a mixture of air and gravel. 'It's bloody lovely to see you again. I was worried you'd taken one look and buggered off for good.'

Her friend Moonpaw was the smarter of the two, with a fetching bandana, sailor's T-shirt and an old man's suit folded up at the legs. She was leaning on her stick. 'Oh, and you've brought your friend.'

'This is Annie!' said Denise happily.

'Hello!' said Annie, thrilled.

'Eh?' said Rainbow, squinting through her, puzzled.

Moonpaw stretched out a heavily bangled hand towards her. 'Come on, my loves, let the dog see the rabbit. We've Bingo to organise.'

They entered the hall through a cloud of smoke that was half joss-stick and half Old Holborn.

In many ways, the sports hall was both beautiful and sad. Signs were nailed across the walls in neatly imposing rows: *Bristol In Bloom: Best Kept Football Pitch 1983, Avon Football Cup Squad 1976, John Noakes opens the Club Room 1973*. Everything tailed off at some point in the 1990s with a team being handed a cup by a long since disgraced chat-show presenter. It all looked terrible.

Moonpaw could sense Annie's disappointment. 'We've seen better days, my child. No one knows we're here any more.' She waved a hand around. 'It's just us two old relics, some hockey sticks, and the Scouts on alternate Tuesdays. But we're going to try and make a comeback.'

'What about the younger members?'

'Ohhhh, bless you,' sighed Moonpaw. 'Time was there were rotas and rosters and club captains and even kit monitors. The cricket club fighting with the football team for Thursday evenings. We even had a little bowls pitch. Happy, happy days. But now the kids just aren't organised.'

Rainbow stopped looking puzzled and joined in. 'No order! Not even a bloody chart.' She wrinkled her nose. 'Now they just turn up and play whenever they damn well feel like it. ' She shook her head, sadly.

'Which isn't so bad, I suppose,' admitted Moonpaw. 'I've always felt we shouldn't be too constraining.' She swept her arms out across the room, and gave an enormous sigh that shook her cleavage, like a dying opera singer. 'But the children! Oh! Free spirits are wonderful, aren't they, but they're so hopeless when it comes to helping out with the facilities. Which is why we do the Bingo. You know – once a month, hoping to raise a bit more.'

'Tell 'em how much you made last time,' she prompted Rainbow.

Rainbow's head swung round vaguely. 'Tell who…? Well, it would be about eight bloody quid, wouldn't it?'

'Eight bloody quid and seven pence, my dears,' corrected Moonpaw sharply. 'That's not going to pay for a new shower block is it?'

'Not even a block of soap and a rusty bucket,' growled Rainbow.

'Kids don't use soap nowadays. It's gel, dear. We'll need dispensers.'

'We can't afford sodding dispensers.' Rainbow shook her head. One of her shawls came loose and she started patting at it uncertainly.

Moonpaw turned to them, her face settled in an ancient calm. 'You see, my children, we can't afford hot water, but we can afford dreams.'

'Oh, we have dreams coming out of our arses,' Rainbow added.

'Quite,' said Moonpaw. 'Now. Let's pop the kettle on.'

'Please,' said Annie. 'Let me!'

Ignoring her, Rainbow shuffled off into the kitchen.

Moonpaw made a face. 'Sorry, my child. She's very set in her ways. Doesn't like change. Not at her age. Lost her fella last year.'

'How long had they been married?' asked Annie dutifully.

'Oh, her husband's still alive, the miserable old swine. No, it was the postman, dear. She's very old fashioned, as I said.'

'Right,' said Annie.

Moonpaw leaned back against an old vaulting horse and coughed. She looked around like a stoned Womble and then smiled her widest smile at Annie. 'Now, my child, Denise here says you've got some exciting new ideas for our little Bingo night.'

She looked as though she was waiting for Annie to say something clever. Annie didn't know what to say. She stared desperately at Denise, who just shook her head and grinned. This was Annie's moment...

From the tiny storeroom at the back of the hall came a rattling of cups.

'Well,' said Annie and then stopped. 'Well... ah, now

bear with me as some of these things are so radical you may find them not radical at all. We're bringing the wheel full circle.'

'Ah, a cycle of change,' said Moonpaw, nodding approvingly. In the distance, Rainbow could be heard banging a kettle down and swearing.

'Real old-fashioned feeling of fun, isn't that right, Denise?' Annie was warming to her subject. 'We're going to put up flyers across the city. We're going to go round the hospital. We're really going to get your event out there. And we're going to do out the hall. Like in a makeover show.'

'I see,' said Moonpaw. 'And how are you going to manage that then?'

It was at this point that Annie remembered she didn't have a bank account. Or any money. And she looked at Denise and then back at Moonpaw's face, interested but sceptical.

Then she remembered the cupboard by the back door, full of old tins of paint and Christmas decorations and fairy lights. Lots and lots of fairy lights. She smiled.

'It's not going to cost a penny,' she said firmly.

'Strictly speaking, isn't that a misuse of NHS property?' asked George.

Mitchell looked up from the photocopier. 'I am doing this for Annie,' he said. 'Photocopying flyers. It's all in a good cause. And tell me,' he smirked, 'what else do you do when you wreck that basement once a month?'

'Ahhh,' said George. 'That's different. That is a community service.'

'As is Bingo,' Mitchell scooped up the flyers and made off. Then he stopped and split the pile in two. 'Here's half.

Go crazy, tiger.'

George stared down at the leaflets in horror. 'Suddenly this is my job?'

'We're doing it for Annie. And Denise. But mostly Annie.'

'Right,' said George, wincing as the lights from the photocopier strobed across his eyes. 'I still feel awful. I just want to go home and crawl into my bed. Or under it. Right now I'm not fussy.'

'And you can.' Mitchell nudged him on the shoulder. 'But first you get to hand out some leaflets and be a hero.'

'I don't want to be a hero,' said George quietly, but Mitchell had gone.

'You did really well,' said Denise. 'That was brilliant! Brilliant!'

They were walking back across the park.

'Do you think?' asked Annie keenly.

'Oh yeah,' Denise beamed. 'You really got those two loves going.'

'Thanks for ambushing me with that,' said Annie.

Denise laughed. 'Sorry about that. Surprise has always been my best weapon. And you've got to admit, it got a lot out of you. Those old hippies just lapped you up.'

'Rainbow ignored me totally,' said Annie. 'Like I wasn't even there.'

'I think she just doesn't like new things, poor dear. But she'll change her tune when we have the best Bingo night ever.' She laughed again. And Annie laughed too.

'This is silly, isn't it?' said Annie. 'What are we doing trying to take over the Bingo at a piss-poor sports club?'

Denise sucked air through her teeth. 'That's not the

spirit, Annie luv. We're getting you out of the house and into Funland. Team Annie! Woo!'

'Right,' said Annie. 'But you're not the one who's going to be spending the evening taking Santas off Christmas decorations.'

They walked on up the park.

Behind them, the two lonely men had been joined by two more who stood there, watching them and sniffing the air.

'Hey!'

Sarah on reception looked up. There was Mitchell. All glamour and shine and a big, big smile. Sourly, she pointed at the queue of people waiting to be seen. 'Not now,' she said. 'Busy.'

'I know!' Mitchell leaned in, smiling widely. 'Kid with an actual saucepan on his head! How classic is that?'

Sarah tried not to smile. 'I'm busy, Mitchell. What do you want?'

'I have come,' said Mitchell, with the air of a man making a really big announcement, 'I have come to spread a little bit of happiness in everyone's lives.'

'Oh really?' said Sarah, carefully unimpressed. 'Are you leaving?'

Mitchell looked at the pretty girl, with her badly ironed clothes and her battered handbag plonked open on the desk, and her look of barely-holding-it-together. And, for an instant, he faltered. And then he thought *No, this is what being human is all about*, and he leaned forward just a little closer and smiled a little wider. 'I wouldn't dream of leaving without you, Sarah.'

Sarah rolled her eyes, and Mitchell took it as encouragement. He plonked some flyers down on the desk.

'I bring you the miracle of Bingo. Can you do us a favour? Hand them out to everyone? Take one yourself. It's just around the corner. Make a night of it. Go on…'

Sarah eyed the flyers and then looked at Mitchell. 'You. Would. Like. Me. To. Give. Patients. Flyers?'

Mitchell nodded like a puppy. 'Yup. Do it, and I will love you for ever. And trust me, that's a very long time.'

'I'll see,' muttered Sarah.

'I'll be there,' said Mitchell. 'Go on. I'll buy you a shandy. You could win a microwave. Imagine that. If you won, I could come over and we could microwave some popcorn and watch that *Sex and the City* movie. Twice, if necessary.'

'Don't push your luck,' said Sarah.

'You'll do it?' Mitchell beamed. 'Thank you!' He planted a kiss on her forehead and turned away, catching the eye of a man with a bandaged arm. 'This woman is the best. She'll make sure you get absolutely the finest drugs.' And with that he was away.

Sarah grimaced at the man with the broken arm, and then picked up the flyer. 'Bingo night?' she said, offering it to him.

UP TO TRICKS

46

'Just popping in to see how things are going,' boomed Denise down the hospital corridor. Behind her were the sounds of the ward. An old lady was crying, someone was shouting, and a nurse could be heard talking crossly on the phone.

That used to be Nina's ward, thought George, sadly. He'd even come to recognise it by the smell – there was a different kind of disinfectant to it. Oh yes.

And then he noticed Denise. Still standing there, leaning against the noticeboard, brown hair swept back, clothes all neat, waiting for an answer. She was smiling which made her look even prettier.

'Uh… do you mind?' George blurted out. 'You're pulling against one of my Bingo posters.' He rested the pile of towels on a desk, and carefully smoothed out the poster.

'Oops,' said Denise, leaning forward. 'Sorry. Didn't mean

to get in the way. You've done marvellous work. They're all over the streets.'

'That'll be Mitchell,' said George. 'He's like a child sometimes.'

'Yeah,' said Denise. 'You two boys are absolute treasures.' Her smile died. 'Do you like me, George?'

'Pardon?' said George, and then stumbled, 'Er, yes.'

'Cos I know what it's like. You've got your routine, and here am I tearing all that apart. And I know how it is. You like a quiet life in. Cups of tea, and *The Real Hustle*, and a nice early night. Am I right?' Denise leaned closer, smiling at him. He could hear her earrings jingling.

'Er, yes, mostly,' replied George, looking down and frantically smoothing out a particularly persistent crease. Trying to pull a corner, his hand brushed Denise's. 'You seem like a… lovely person. And Annie likes you. Which is very nice.'

'Right,' Denise stood back and folded her arms. 'But…?'

'Oh,' said George, not looking up from the poster. 'Look, do you mind? This is personal.'

Denise grinned. 'Let me guess. You've got a secret girlfriend you're hiding from me. Have you locked her in the cellar?'

'Sort of,' muttered George, agonised. 'I think we've split up. Well, we may have. I'm not sure. She's gone away.'

'Sorry about that,' said Denise. 'Sorry in all sorts of ways.'

'And, if you don't mind, I find you a bit full on.' With a huff of wounded dignity, George turned his back to her and pinned the poster back up.

'Noted,' said Denise.

There was a silence. George finished putting up the

poster and turned back, blushing slightly. 'Not that I'm against, ah, feminism and a woman saying what she wants. No. But you're very… out there.' George attempted a mime, appeared to be describing breasts, and stopped.

Denise giggled. 'I'm just fun, George. You should try it some time.' She walked away, waving over her shoulder.

'I am fun,' said George in an injured tone. 'I am quite fun quite a lot of the time.'

But Denise had vanished.

He found Mitchell slumped in the canteen, head cradled in his hands.

'I thought you were feeling better,' he said accusingly.

Mitchell shook his head and winced. 'I was, but then… I dunno… a few minutes ago… it was like hair of the dog. No offence.'

'None taken,' said George, sitting down and looking at him, concerned. 'Are you all right?'

Mitchell raised his head. 'It's like I'm drunk. Thank God I'm not about to perform keyhole surgery, eh?' He stood up, unsteadily. 'Right. Better get on before McGough catches me drunk in charge of a mop. I'm going to go and empty some bins. And try not to throw up in any of them.'

'Cool,' said George. He was about to say something, but instead said, 'What about a mixed grill when we get home? Or hamburgers?'

'Pizza,' muttered Mitchell. 'I need pizza. Really cheap pizza coated with mystery meat and barbeque sauce.'

'Oh yes,' said George, nodding. 'That's absolutely what we're having. And an old film.'

'A really old film,' said Mitchell, staggering a little as he left the room.

George sighed, left alone in the canteen. Then he smiled. 'Lightweight,' he said.

George pottered down a corridor and headed towards the locker room. He couldn't wait to get home. It had been a long, tiring day. He was shattered.

He still noticed two things, though. The first was Mitchell, standing at the end of a corridor, looking terrible, and arguing quietly with a small crowd of about half a dozen people. Some were young, some were older, but they were all thin, and they all glanced sourly at George as he passed.

The second was on a list. A tiny piece of hospital paperwork. Not even the sheet on the clipboard he was supposed to be looking at. But he noticed a name on that list. And he thought, 'Odd. Well, that explains one thing…'

Then he went home and ordered pizza.

Mitchell descended on the staff room, littering it with flyers. A slightly tired, fat orderly picked up a leaflet and stared at it. 'Bingo?'

Mitchell nodded gravely. 'Oh yes. Can I tempt you, Mossy?'

Mossy stared at the flyer and then narrowly at Mitchell. 'You want me to come along to this when you've ducked out of the bowling team the last three sessions?'

'Ah,' said Mitchell, embarrassed. 'Yes. Well, come along and I promise that next time, I will most definitely consider coming bowling. Go, team!'

He beat a quick retreat.

Annie had filled the living room with tinsel. An inflatable

Santa bounced around.

'My word!' said George. 'How did you manage that?'

'I know!' Annie was delighted, all smiles. 'Look! Santa's filled with ghost breath!'

'Wow,' said George. 'Both tasteless and impossible. Brilliant. What's all this for, please?'

Annie folded her arms. 'It's for the Bingo. We're redecorating the sports hall.'

'Ah, of course, for the Bingo. Everything's for the Bingo.' George sank down wearily onto a chair.

'Denise says it's a good idea.'

'Denise… yes,' said George.

Annie was painting a Bingo number on a bauble. She put it carefully down on the table and looked at George. 'What aren't you saying? Are you jealous of her?'

George folded his arms. 'No. Well, no. Not really. It's just suddenly everything is Denise. Denise this, Denise that. Even Mitchell is besotted with her. You know… she's only been around a couple of days. And suddenly it's like we're All Denise All The Time.'

'She's always been a bit like that,' Annie told him, a little defensive. 'And she's been working as a holiday rep. That's what she does – parties and fun and getting along with people. You have been on holiday, yes?'

'Of course I've been on holiday,' said George. 'But I always avoided the rep. Picked out my own hotels, you know. I preferred to be left to my own devices. I don't really like organised fun.'

'You could never tell,' said Annie sourly and picked up the bauble again.

'What's that supposed to mean?' asked George.

'Oh nothing,' said Annie. 'I'm just surprised you aren't

finding the whole idea of Bingo a little racy.'

There was a tight silence for a second. Then George coughed. 'If you'll excuse me,' he said with dignity, 'I have pizza to order. Stuffed crust, actually.'

Annie didn't look up from painting the bauble. 'Go crazy, big boy. Get a side order of coleslaw.'

Dr McGough made his way across the dark car park, looking nervously around him. Last to leave again. He'd tried to improve the lighting, but he still felt afraid. He'd meant to leave earlier, but had been caught up in a budgeting meeting. Trying not to show his nervousness, he reached his car, felt in his pocket for keys and then stiffened. Someone was standing behind him.

'Don't turn around,' said a woman's voice, sounding in his ear without any breath hitting the back of his neck.

McGough tried to see a reflection in his car windscreen, but couldn't. He just stood there, feeling absolute and utter terror.

'It's you again, isn't it?' He tried to sound casual but failed.

'Dr McGough, who else creeps up on you in the car park?' The woman's voice managed to be richly amused without being in any way less chilling. There was the crunch of an expensive boot, and suddenly she stood before him.

She towered over him, the streetlight absorbed by her ebony black skin. An old army greatcoat was tailored to her amazing figure. She was smiling at him, and it was quite the worst smile he had ever seen.

'Good evening,' she said. 'My name is Death.' She laughed. 'Well, actually it's Olive, but Death is better, no?'

'Are you going to kill me?' McGough heard his voice ask,

and honestly, desperately wished he'd said something else.

She shrugged. 'Would you like me to, Declan?'

'No,' he said firmly. 'I know what you are.'

She arched an eyebrow. 'Then say it. Go on.'

McGough looked into her eyes. 'No,' he croaked eventually.

She shrugged. 'OK. Suit yourself. Now, tell me, brave doctor – did you follow up my little tip about Leo Willis?'

McGough nodded. 'I did. It took a bit of effort, but I managed to obtain a sample of his blood.'

Olive narrowed her eyes. 'A sample? Come on, handsome. You can do better than that.'

'Fine,' said McGough. 'Two samples. One for me, and one for you.'

Olive nodded. 'That's better. Do you have it on you?'

McGough rummaged in his coat pocket and produced the blood sample. 'It's from the autopsy,' he said, aware his voice sounded like it was bleating. 'Is it of any use to you now? It's dead blood, isn't it?'

Olive took the test tube and tapped it with a beautifully painted nail. 'Oh, we have our own scientists, Dr McGough. We're as interested in poor Leo Willis's nasty, nasty blood as you are. But for different reasons.' She held it up to the light. 'Funny, isn't it?' she said. 'It looks the same. It even…' She sniffed. 'Yes, it smells the same. But you and I know it's lethal to my kind.' She smiled and slipped the vial into her coat pocket. 'Ah well,' she said. 'Thank you. I'd better not keep you.'

Relief flooded through McGough, but he didn't dare let himself relax. 'That's it?' he gasped.

'Stupid question to ask a vampire,' tutted Olive.

'But you know the work I'm engaged in,' stammered

McGough. 'You know what I could do with the other sample…'

Olive looked at him as though considering the question, and her exquisite smile faded slightly before coming back stronger than ever. 'Of course I do. And I know why you're doing it. I even have a certain amount of sympathy. But…' She laid a long hand very lightly on his shoulder, and McGough felt the heat draw out of his body. 'I don't think it's going to work. Sorry. Nice idea, though.'

'But you can't argue with the science!' protested McGough.

'Yes I can. I'm a myth.' Olive laughed again, and showed off her perfect teeth. 'But I'll tell you what. I am going to do two things. Firstly, I'm going to leave town.' She started to walk away from him into the night. 'And secondly, I'm going to let you live.'

Then she was gone.

Mitchell stared at the thin wodge of flyers he still had to get rid of. He noticed two teenage girls leaning against the playground wall. 'Ladies!' he said, 'I don't suppose I can interest you in an evening of Bingo, can I?'

The two girls looked back at him, sullenly.

'Oh, go on,' said Mitchell. 'There's lots of prizes. Some of them neither meat nor wicker. It's exciting.' He waggled an eyebrow encouragingly.

The two girls glared back. The thinner one with more make-up took a flyer sceptically. 'Really? Bingo? And what are the prizes again?'

Mitchell looked at the lipstick on her and the make-up. How old was she? Fifteen? He tried to ignore the smell of youth coming off her. Yeah. Just keep it neutral and polite. He reeled off a list of prizes from a flyer. 'Cutlery, microwave, organic sausages…'

The girl peered down at the flyer then looked him in the eyes. 'And what about you?' she asked. 'Can we win you?'

I am going home, thought Mitchell.

George stood in the hall ordering pizza on the phone. And he wondered. First Bingo – what next? He was amazed Denise hadn't taken Annie shopping for a clothing makeover. He supposed he should be grateful for small mercies. All they had to do was get through the next couple of days and then it would be Bingo, and everything would be fine. Back to normal.

Mitchell slumped in and picked up a slice of cold pizza. It flopped about in his hands like a dead fish. He groaned and rolled it up and started tearing chunks off of it.

'I. Am. Exhausted,' he sighed.

George opened an eye. He'd been dozing. 'You've missed the lottery show,' he said. 'It was a rollover week.'

'Did we win?'

'I keep getting very close,' said Annie, pottering through from the kitchen. She handed Mitchell a glass of wine and he drained it. 'Of course, I can never really claim the prize, can I?'

'No,' said George. 'But we could split it.'

'Lovely,' said Annie. 'Why?'

'To stop them asking questions. You don't want us telling Thunderball you're a ghost, now, do you?'

The doorbell rang.

'If it's a Jehovah's Witness, bring him in, I'm still hungry,' called Mitchell.

George opened the door. It was Denise.

'Oh God,' he said. And then coughed. 'Hello.'

'Hi gorgeous!' she said, grabbing him in a hug. For the first time, George noticed her perfume. It was, he thought, a bit much. Nice, but a bit much. Summed her up.

Awkwardly trying to return her kiss on both cheeks without getting a mouthful of hair, George leaned back into the living room. 'Oh look, everyone – it's Denise.'

Mitchell glanced round, livening up a bit.

Annie rushed through carrying a box full of Bingo balls.

'We're going to end up going for a drink, aren't we?' sighed George.

They went to a nice bar by the Corn Exchange in the centre of town. On their way down, they passed the fountain, now bubbling over with washing-up liquid. Groups of thin people were lounging around. And Annie – are you reading this, Annie? We're coming for you.

Denise muttered to Mitchell, 'Lot of those emo kids around aren't there?'

Mitchell jammed his hands in his pocket and strode ahead, hustling them towards the bar. It was crowded. George looked behind them and noticed the groups picking themselves up off the park benches and trailing behind them at a distance.

'Can we have a word?' asked George at the bar.

Mitchell sighed, trying to get the barman's attention. 'Well, yes, we're having a word now aren't we?'

'Yes but, I am serious,' said George. 'Haven't you noticed that wherever we go there are vampires around at the moment?'

'Can't say that I have,' sighed Mitchell.

'Really? You're not at all astonished at the remarkable number of pale people wearing black and looking artistic we keep bumping into?'

Mitchell turned around slightly and the barman sailed past. He groaned. 'Fine, yes, fine, there are a few more... well... some... around.'

'It's you, isn't it?' said George.

'What?' gasped Mitchell, missing the barman's attention again. 'How can you say that?'

'You're king of the vampires now. You're their dark lord aren't you?'

'No! It doesn't work like that!' groaned Mitchell. 'And even if I was, I'd only be the dark lord of Avon and Somerset.'

'Well, that's all right, then,' said George. A barmaid wandered past and looked at him. 'Two pints of bitter and a white wine, please,' he said, and Mitchell scowled.

George turned round to gloat and discovered that Mitchell had gone.

'This seat taken?' Mitchell asked.

He was in a quiet corner of the pub. Betty and Arnold the pensioner vampires sat there, nursing pints and dabbing at the remains of a packet of prawn cocktail crisps. Betty's shopping trolley nestled by the table, canvas sides squirming only slightly.

'Not at all, dear, sit yourself down,' said Betty, grinning.

'Don't be so soft,' muttered Arnold. 'The bugger's older than we are.'

Betty licked her fingers. 'Yes, dear, but he's got his youth. We're in our prime.'

Mitchell dragged the chair forward across the pub carpet.

'What are you two doing here?'

'Just out for a stroll. You know, taking the walk for a dog.' Arnold indicated the canvas trolley with a nudge.

'It's about all we can manage, dear, what with our teeth.'

'Sometimes I don't know why our Christopher turned us,' sighed Arnold.

'Don't speak about him like that!' Betty put down her stout and scowled at her husband, truly cross. 'He was a good son, he was. Couldn't face the idea of losing his own dear parents.'

'Wish he'd done it twenty bloody years sooner,' sighed Arnold, coughing a bit.

'Oh, we mustn't grumble. We've the National Health, thank goodness.'

And a very surprised GP, thought Mitchell.

Betty sighed. 'It was so good of him. But then, just after he'd turned us, we never saw him again. Poor Christopher. I hope he's out there somewhere.'

Mitchell coughed uneasily.

Arnold looked at him. 'She made me go and see Mr Herrick. I didn't want to bother him, but he told me the lad was doing well. He'd look into it.'

'And we never heard a thing,' said Betty. 'Not that we're complaining.'

'No,' said Arnold, and sipped his pint.

Mitchell changed the subject. 'And you're here tonight. Why?'

Betty glanced up at the room. 'Such a lovely evening dear.'

'Lovely,' agreed Arnold.

'Can't you just smell it in the air? It's like summer, or fabric softener. Smashing.'

Mitchell indicated the other customers. 'And you're not the only vampires in the bar. You do know that?'

'Well, that's as may be,' said Arnold. 'But we're not nosy. We keep ourselves to ourselves. Don't pry. Now I know Mr Herrick liked vampires to keep away from the rest… but that was then, if you see what I mean.'

And Betty's little old hands rested on Mitchell's. 'But you're not like that, are you, dear? You're not going to object to two harmless old folks having a quiet drink.'

The canvas bag whined quietly. Mitchell stood up and walked away. Something was wrong.

GANDHI'S TEA

80

The next day, George had a plan. Originally the plan hadn't included leaning over the sink seeing whether or not he was going to throw up his breakfast, but now he was definitely sticking to the plan.

He stood in the hospital corridor, waiting round the corner from the swing doors, counted down, and then pushed through.

'Oh!' he said, feigning astonishment. 'Fancy bumping into you!'

'Well, look who it isn't,' said Denise, folding her arms and staring at George. 'What a startling surprise.'

'What a coincidence,' echoed George, wilting slightly under Denise's gaze.

'Yes,' continued Denise, frowning slightly. 'Considering I could see you peering round the corner waiting for me to turn up, yes.'

'Oh,' said George. 'Oh.' He looked down at the lino guiltily. He really should get around to mopping it later. Then he looked back at Denise. 'Hello,' he said.

'Hi!' Denise waved, clutching sunglasses and a posh coffee in the other hand.

'Do you come here often?' he asked.

She rolled her eyes. 'Yes, as a matter of fact.'

'And what's a lovely girl like you doing in a place like this?' he pressed on.

Denise muttered something and then looked at him. 'I'm an outpatient here, George. That's why I'm back in Bristol. I suppose it's easier I tell you than have you break the Data Protection Act.'

George shrugged, failing to look casual. 'I just saw your name on some paperwork, and I thought I'd make sure…'

Denise leaned back against the wall and sighed. 'You're such an old woman. Look, I'm just getting some treatment. Perfectly routine, just the kind of thing you can't quite get on the Greek Medical Service. Hot doctors, oh, they've got plenty of those, but they're not exactly cutting edge.'

'I see…?' George gestured.

Denise laughed. 'Women's troubles, George.'

George blushed. 'Oh.' He leaned forward. 'It's just that you're seeing… Dr McGough.'

'I am,' sighed Denise.

George's voice became most confidential. 'Well, he's not a very nice person.'

'I don't care,' laughed Denise. 'He's a very good doctor, and that's all I need. Quick MOT, repeat prescription, back out in the sun. Job done.' She smiled.

'I was just…' he said.

'I know,' she said. 'And it's probably sweet of you. But it's also a bit creepy.'

'Yes,' admitted George. 'You're not the first woman to tell me that.'

Denise raised an eyebrow. 'Right, I'm off to help Annie decorate her hut. Maybe a drink after work?'

George paled. 'Tiny bit of sick in my mouth,' he whispered.

Denise poked him in the ribs. 'Oh, you'll be fine. You and Mitchell are just such lightweights. You need to come out to Mykonos sometime. We'll teach you to drink! You need some fun, and Mitchell could do with staking out in the sun.'

'Um,' said George.

'See you later, alligator,' said Denise, and sailed off down the corridor.

George looked at the grubby floor and then back at her, and went off to get a mop.

Mitchell stared at him in horror across the canteen. 'We can't go out drinking again. I'll phone Amnesty.'

'She is making us!' protested George.

'That woman… In my home village they'd have thrown her down a well by now. This is just cos you fancy her.'

'I do not!' George flushed slightly. 'It is because she is helping Annie out of her shell.'

Mitchell made yap yap yap motions with his hand. 'Whatever.'

'Look,' said George. 'This is important. There's something Denise has not been telling us. She's a patient at this hospital.'

'So?' Mitchell started to load chips from George's plate onto his own, fitting them between two buttered slices of bread. 'Lots of people get ill,' he said through a full mouth.

'But she's not told Annie.'

'So?' Mitchell shrugged. 'I didn't hear Annie telling her she was a ghost, did I? Friends keep stuff from each other. That's how they stay friends.'

'Right,' said George, uncertainly. 'Um, do you keep stuff from me?'

'All the time,' said Mitchell gravely.

'Such… Such as?' George looked at him urgently.

Mitchell opened his mouth, paused and then smiled. 'If I told you, I wouldn't be keeping it from you, now would I?'

George blinked. 'This is some trick to make me all paranoid, isn't it?' He narrowed his eyes.

'Or your breath could be really bad.' Mitchell shrugged again. 'Did Denise say what it was?'

'Not really…' George looked up from breathing on his hands.

'Then best not to ask,' said Mitchell. 'Women like their privacy. It's like me talking to you when you're trying to take a slash. These chips are gorgeous.'

'Really?' George's voice was cold. 'But she's seeing Dr McGough. And I don't trust him.'

'Right.' Mitchell stared at him coolly. 'And a porter is planning on a hate campaign against the new hospital administrator?'

'I might be.' George's voice was faint. 'There's something about that man. He's… shifty.'

'"Shifty"?' Mitchell smiled. 'Are his eyes too close together?'

'Well, as it happens, they are.'

Mitchell threw a chip at him.

*

Denise sat in the kitchen while Annie hurled herself around. 'Come on, darling! The least you can do is let me help. Smells gorgeous. Surely I can just do the washing up or something.'

'No no!' Annie's voice came from inside the oven. 'This is brilliant. I haven't cooked like this for ages.'

'You know,' said Denise, 'most people would be happy with making a few egg and cress sandwiches and maybe defrosting some sausage rolls.'

'Oh no!' Annie spun round, the oven door seeming to slam itself shut. Denise blinked. 'These people are getting homemade quiche and vol-au-vents and profiteroles.'

Denise giggled. 'You never did things by half.'

'I'm a domestic goddess,' said Annie proudly, and then sagged a little and sat down, laying her oven-gloved hands on the table. 'Or at least I would have been. If it hadn't been for Owen…'

'Do you want to talk about it?' asked Denise.

He pushed me down the stairs, said he would have me exorcised, and shagged Janey 'Tango' Harris. We are not talking about it.

'No,' said Annie.

Denise drew off an oven glove and took Annie's hand. 'Then don't think about it. Move on. Enjoy life. It's short enough, God knows.' She lifted the hand and mock-slapped Annie around the face with it. 'And stop thinking that everyone is out to get you.'

'Yeah,' said Annie quietly. She'd got a letter that morning. She'd been quite excited to get post, even if it was from the *Reader's Digest*. It began: '*Dear Annie, you could have already won a million years of suffering…*'

'Right,' said Denise. 'Shall we take some of this stuff down to the sports hall and get ready for tomorrow? Those biddies will be there. Lord Almighty, maybe we should have a drink before we go there. I swear they'd burn me at the stake if they had the chance.'

'I like them. Well, I like Moonpaw. Rainbow's still ignoring me.'

'Old women are funny that way. Don't like anything new. Talcum powder and weak pelvic floors, that's what causes it,' said Denise. 'Come along, love. Chop chop! I'm taking the boys out later.'

'Are you trying to break them?'

Denise shrugged. 'It's my way. I'm on holiday. Call it research for making sure everyone has a really brilliant night tomorrow. We're taking out a tonne of flyers and we're going to plaster the town. It's student night tonight – who's not going to come along for the quiche tomorrow?'

Much, much later, George and Denise got jacket potatoes from Jason Doner Van and took them to the suspension bridge.

'Should you, ah, be drinking in your condition?' asked George.

'I'm not pregnant!' laughed Denise. 'And stop fishing. Private.'

'Sure,' said George, swaying a little.

They passed a sign for the Samaritans saying *Troubled? Please Call Us*.

Denise breathed in the air. 'It's brilliant up here. It's cold, but that kind of suits it, you know.'

George nodded. 'It's the Avon Gorge. There used to be a little cable railway taking people down to the bottom. It was the second most popular tourist attraction in the Victorian Era.'

'Shut up, George,' said Denise, laughing. 'I'm trying to enjoy my spud. You're taking all the romance out of the evening. Here we are, two young people stood on a bridge by the moonlight. Anything could happen.'

'Fair enough,' said George, glancing furtively up at the moon. 'I'm all for romance.'

'Are you, George?' teased Denise. 'It's just sometimes… Well, it's as though you don't like having fun. You know, normally… fun is like my superpower. But with you… it's like you enjoy being miserable. Just like you're punishing yourself. You should live a little, you know. You're only put on this Earth once, and it's not as though you're some kind of mass murderer. You're just a nice boy with a cute smile and you should make the most of it. Now what's up? I bet it's your girlfriend. I'm right, I know it.'

There was a pause. The wind twisted its way through the cables around them which creaked like an old ship's mast.

'She left me,' said George. 'Her name was Nina and we were living together, and then it all got a bit much and she just walked out. Recently.'

'Right,' said Denise. 'I'm sorry.'

They stood there, George scraping the plastic fork around his rapidly cooling beans. 'And it was all my fault,' he said.

'How?' asked Denise. She stepped a bit closer to him. 'I can't see you being a bad boy.'

George breathed in deeply. 'I was a shit,' he said, quietly. They stood there a bit longer. 'I did something really terrible to her. And then several more really terrible things, actually. All because I was so sorry. I really loved her.' He sniffed. 'She had great toothpaste.'

Denise bopped him gently on the nose. 'Poor George,' she said. 'I can't imagine you being a bastard.'

'Yes. Well. I surprised myself,' he said. He turned away and pointed down to the gorge. 'Do you know, when most people throw themselves off here, they don't die at once? The fall doesn't kill them. Apparently, it's the mud. When the tide's out at night, you see, they break their legs when they land. And they lie there, having second thoughts, stuck in the mud in terrible pain, and then the tide comes back in and they slowly drown.'

Denise stared at him, open-mouthed. 'Way to change the subject, George,' she whistled.

George carried on, not looking at her, just babbling away. 'Sometimes they don't die. They get help, they ring someone, they're rescued and they're brought in. And we see them in the hospital. And I've never dared to come right out and ask it. You know – they decided to kill themselves, right? To jump over the edge. They've actually gone through with it. The most courageous thing they've ever done in their life. And it didn't work – instead they just got a whole load of misery and shit. And I want to ask them how it feels.'

Denise swallowed, and peered over the edge. 'You know, there's people down there now,' she said.

'What?' George crossed to the barrier.

'Yeah,' she said. 'Standing on the mud, a small crowd of them. Looking up. Do you think it's some kind of Samaritans Rescue Squad?'

George squinted. 'No. They're not an ambulance crew. They look more like bikers.'

'Oh yeah,' Denise shivered. 'Isn't that creepy? Standing on the riverbed at night looking up at us. Are they waiting for us to jump or just watching us?'

George stared down at the figures, mostly in black, standing there, watching. He shivered.

Denise had stepped closer to him. 'So, shall we jump then?' she asked.

'Don't joke about it,' said George.

Denise let her breath out slowly as though thinking about something. 'Look,' she said, 'I've always found shy men attractive. And… you know, perhaps I could show you how to live a little.'

George drew back. 'No,' he said, sadly. 'Please no. You don't understand. I'm not good. I thought I could be… that I might be able to… but… Listen,' he breathed. 'I… I'm bad news, Denise. You really don't want what I've got.'

'Is that so?' said Denise, and she laughed too. But this time her laugh was a little sad, and her eyes were shining. 'And perhaps, George, you don't want what I've got…'

Intermission

WHAT I DID ON MY HOLIDAYS

Annie

The last time I went on holiday, it was with Owen. It was
kind of a trial run for the honeymoon, I guess. He wanted
somewhere with a bar, I wanted a beach. He wanted surfing,
I wanted a bit of culture. I know that sounds awful now,
but really, we weren't that incompatible. Anyway, the Isle
of Wight seemed like a good idea.

Oddly, he got terribly ill and I was fine. He spent most
of his time in the hotel, throwing up. He told me to go off
and have fun. So I got to wander around. I even hired a
bike, went swimming, made some friends, ate some really
disgusting stuff… You know, most of the things we'd been
planning on doing together.

He just lay there for days. He looked dead, ashen and
sweating wrapped up in a hotel sheet. I was trying to get
him to drink some coke, but he wasn't having any of it. He

just stared at me. 'Annie,' he laughed, 'you're indestructible. It's like you're going to live for ever.'

And I kissed him. Which is funny, really.

George

The last time I went on holiday, it was to Scotland. It was a mini-break kind of thing. Walking and so on. I'd even loved the sleeper train on the way up, travelling at five miles an hour through empty wet Scottish highlands. I was on the top bunk, proving I was a man. My girlfriend, Julia, was underneath. We held hands and giggled. We got off at a station somewhere and took a taxi. And the castle was everything I'd hoped for. Old and desolate and crumbling. Lovely breakfast and then a nice long walk around the lake, or into the woods.

Julia was really, really bored. Just slumping around the castle, reading Agatha Christie and looking at the rain. But I liked it. I couldn't hide how much I liked it. Everything felt so fresh and close to nature and fun.

'Have I brought you on the worst holiday ever?' I asked one night. She had given up trying to find all the bones in her trout and was instead picking at the vegetables on the side. She put down her fish knife and looked at me.

'No, George,' she said. 'Well, yes, George. But the thing is... you're happy. You're like some kind of nature boy. It's like you're 8 again and playing in a tree house.'

I pointed my fork at her. 'Do you know, that's the one thing I was thinking. This place really lacks a tree house.'

She giggled. I liked making her laugh.

'I found some owl pellets today. You can unwrap them and, and it's like a little inside-out mouse – skeleton perfectly preserved! It's all in the right order, and stuffed full of mouse fur. It's brilliant.'

She looked at me, ashen. 'Please don't tell me you've got one on you. Not at the table, George.'

I shook my head solemnly. 'No. And I washed my hands. Twice.'

We ate on for a bit. And then she smiled. 'I am having a good time, you know.'

'Good.' I said. And I meant it. She was so beautiful. I worried at any moment that that would be it. You know, that she'd dump me. Of course, at a castle in the middle of nowhere, it would be unlikely. But still.

'Would you like to take a walk after dinner?' I asked. 'You know, I was thinking. Well, we could try and see some more of those owls. Just to watch something hunt by the light of the full moon. You know. Romantic.'

Julia smiled and squeezed my hand. 'No, George. You go off. Have fun. For the first time in my life, I think I'm outsmarting Hercule Poirot. I'll be in bed when you get back. Just make sure you wash your hands.'

I never did get back. I went out for that walk. And Derek, one of the other guests came with me. I was a little bit worried about him. It wasn't just that he was American. You know, there was something about him a bit... well, it's not that I've never had a problem with that kind of... live and let live and all. It was just a bit awkward the way he smiled, and there was me thinking, *Is he suddenly going to launch himself on me in the woods?* Ironically, it was Derek who was the prey that night. Poor Derek. I don't think he even much liked the walk. Then he got himself torn apart by a werewolf. And I lost everything that night.

That's the last time I went on holiday.

*

Denise

The hot Greek doctor shrugged regretfully, and I wondered
how much time he spent at the gym.

'So it's some kind of food poisoning? Zorba's Revenge?'
I asked.

'Not quite, madam,' he said, his English old-fashioned.
'It's what-you-say… blood sickness? A virus of the blood.'

I suddenly felt a little ill. 'Not like…'

He shook his head. 'Oh no no no. These days we can
manage hepatitis and even HIV, even on this island. What
you have, it is more obscure. Strangely, the monks here,
they have records of it going back centuries. They call it the
Taint – yes, that is almost it, I am certain. But I am afraid
that you have caught it.'

'And there's a cure?'

He shook his head. 'Forgive me, I must speak carefully.
My English…' Again, an apologetic shrug and those lovely
blue eyes. 'Please do not be worried. Let me just say that
it is… manageable. And rare. Very rare. And that means
that… I have spoken to a friend from medical school. She
is in your Harley Street, and she has put me in touch with
someone. He may be able to help, in fact. He was very
interested, and I even told him about the monks. It makes
him… ah, sympathetique, yes? But it would require travel.
Tell me, madam… Do you know Bristol?'

Mitchell

'You'll do it for me,' said Herrick. He was a small man. Bad
breath, even for a vampire. 'It's a bit gothic, I know, but
sometimes it's important to set an example.'

And, at the time, you know, back then, I kind of got it. All
that insane cruelty.

Christopher and I were tiptoeing around this basement flat in Clifton. He was a bit weedy for a vampire. Real mummy's boy. They even said he'd turned his parents. He'd been a bookshop owner before stumbling across Justine in an alleyway. 'He had a bow tie,' she'd gasped. 'I couldn't resist turning him. Groovy!' But that was the Sixties. Back then we all did silly things, and Clifton – oh you could still pick up some great flats there for a song. It was how Herrick was keeping himself going back then. Smart guy, always had been. If I'd thought about it, I'd have been getting some property, but there he was. Some people even blamed him for the one-way system. That was Herrick all over – a little bit of petty cruelty.

So... I was showing Christopher around the flat. 'I've told everyone I'm on holiday,' he'd said. 'But how strange sneaking around Bristol. And you say Herrick wants us to stay in this flat for a couple of days?'

I shrugged. 'He's not been specific. Not really.'

Christopher turned to me. 'Funny. It's like when I was young... did you used to go on holiday to the bottom of the garden? Dad would help me put up the tent, and Mum would make sandwiches, and off we'd go... I guess, you know, if they'd let me join the Scouts it would have been different, but Mum didn't want me getting into trouble.'

'No,' I said, thinking of something else.

'So here we are, you and me, going on holiday in our home town. Maybe I'll send the folks a postcard.' He giggled.

'Christopher—' I began, but then stopped. He'd found the door.

'What's down here?' he'd asked. 'You know, when this is done up, it'll be lovely. So much space.'

He went through the door, flicking on an old light switch. A bare bulb swung around below along with a damp smell. He went down the old staircase.

'It's the cellar,' I said.

'I've always wanted a cellar,' he said. 'For my train set, really. But I guess also for wine. Isn't that a nice undead thing? You can really lay down some good wine.'

We walked through the cellar which went right the way under the house. And then we reached a corner.

'Oh,' said Christopher, puzzled. 'What's this?'

I shrugged. 'Another cellar.' I handed him the torch I'd brought, and we went down these stairs. Actual stone now. There was a smell to them. A smell of... no, wait, he'd get it. Let him work it out.

We were in the cellar beneath.

'Oh,' he said. 'Golly, it's like the Pharaoh's tomb. Who'd have thought... It's really massive. What a treasure. I can see why Herrick's so keen to have someone look after the property. Is there another...?'

He scampered on ahead, laughing with delight when he found the next stone staircase and the third cellar.

'This must go right down into the hillside,' he gasped. 'Imagine that! Imagine how deep it goes.'

'No,' I said. 'This is as far down as it goes.'

'Still, this is quite something.' He was really relishing it. 'Oh Mitchell, thank you, thank you. You're a real mate to show me something like this.'

I looked at him. I'd have lit a cigarette, only the air was so heavy. 'You do know what this place is, don't you?'

'Oh, of course,' he said airily. 'It's an old slave cellar. I wondered when I saw the house. An old merchant's house – but to find the cellars intact! Most of them have been sealed up. It's not fashionable, you know, to remind people that there's all this down here. Why…' and he gasped, 'there's still manacles here in the wall! Imagine that.' Then his face changed. It sharpened. And he looked at me. 'Oh Mitchell, manacles. We're going to have so much fun! This is going to be the best holiday ever!'

His torch swung away, and he didn't catch the look on my face or see the crowbar coming at his head.

When he came to, he stared at me, sleepily, shaking his hand in the manacles. 'Why, Mitchell!' he laughed, actually laughed. 'Is this some kind of joke?'

I shook my head. 'Sorry, Christopher. It's Herrick.'

'Herrick?' He laughed again. 'What do you mean?'

'It's the children. He warned you to steer clear of the children.'

'Oh that.' Christopher actually managed to wave a casual manacle. 'But they're just so…' He breathed exultantly. 'Herrick – he understands.'

'Oh, he understands. But he warned you,' I told him. 'Too many children, too much attention. He said you should have stuck to pensioners.'

Christopher laughed again. 'That's a bit cruel. So this is a big thing, then? And you're putting the frighteners on me?'

I shook my head. 'Not on you. I don't care about you.'

'That's a relief,' said Christopher. 'For a minute there…'

'It's about frightening everyone else.'

'What…?' said Christopher.

And I turned on my heel and left him. I went up the stairs, and I fetched the bricks and the cement and I listened to his cries as I carefully filled in the passage down to the bottom cellar.

He called my name at first, and then, as his cries faded away, he called for his mother.

I couldn't hear him at all when I walked back up into the flat and locked the cellar door.

TURN OF THE SCREW

62

Denise woke up. Her head hurt, and for a moment she couldn't remember where she was. A squinting eye told her it was pretty much the same shitty Travelodge she'd been in for the last week.

She looked at her watch. She was going to be late. Sod it, let the man wait for once. Then she noticed her arm. She'd scratched herself in the night and the little tracks of blood had made bright scarlet scabs. She stared at them, fascinated and appalled. She rubbed the surface of her arm, watching a drop of blood well out slowly. It looked bright and real against the antiseptic pastel of the hotel room.

She watched it run slowly, gently down her arm, appalled by it.

Then she remembered that she'd told George. She'd been so drunk she'd told George. What a stupid, stupid thing to say. She stared at her mobile, wondering if she'd missed calls from him. She remembered the last time she'd got that drunk, desperately trying to fend off some bloke in a bar in London who just wouldn't take No for an answer.

'Piss off, I'm dying,' she'd said, hoping that would end it all. That he'd just go away. Instead, he'd crumpled like wet bog roll. Talk of magic and hope and last chances. And the look of endless pity in his eyes... So she'd kissed him and told him he was sweet and got a cab home, and he'd rung her three times in the taxi. 'Are you OK? Are you OK? I need to check that you're OK...' he'd said each time and she'd groaned and chewed gum and swigged down water and listened to him drivel on. And then the *We need to talk* and *I'm there for you* texts and the calls she just let ring out.

She'd felt stupid and silly and had vowed never to let it happen again.

Nope, from then on until the end it was going to be just her. Well, just her and some nice fat pills from the NHS washed down with... well, whatever. Cos all of that stuff about 'recommended units' and so on was suddenly meaningless. 'Are there any side effects?' she'd asked at the start.

The reply had brought her up sharp. 'Well, any side effects are long term, and that's really not where we're looking at the moment.' Suddenly the room had seemed very small and stuffy and she'd wanted to run.

At least there was nothing from George. At least he understood. He'd backed off. Which was both nice and also made him a little bit of a shit. But she guessed, you know – hospital porter. Probably trained to ignore people crying as they were wheeled down corridors or sat in their own mess. Just a tight little smile and a look as bored as the guy behind the counter at Starbucks. But no, that wasn't George.

He'd blinked and he'd looked sad and he'd stopped eating his spud. She felt such an idiot for telling him.

'And that,' she muttered as she staggered across the hotel carpet, 'is why we don't tell people we're dying when we're drunk.'

Anyway here she was, another morning after, running late for her appointment. Big day ahead. She necked a pill, swigged down some water and then went and stood under the shower, swearing at herself.

It had been a long day, but it had been worth it. Annie took a last look at the sports hall. There were neat rows of tables laid out ready. A curtain shimmered across the stage, and a glitter ball spun steadily around the room, casting the prize pedestal in a shimmering glow. A bar stood stocked at the back and, next to it, a trestle table heaving with food. 'Individually folded paper napkins!' sighed Annie happily to herself.

Denise was wearing an incredibly low-slung dress that made the most of her breasts. Her hair was done in elaborate curls and she was wearing a sparkling bow tie. She came in through the sports hall doors with Moonpaw and Rainbow. All three cried out in surprise and delight.

'Bloody Nora!' swore Rainbow.

'Now that!' Denise gasped, 'is what I call a buffet. Good enough to eat! I am starving.'

She reached out to grab a sausage roll, but Moonpaw slapped her back. 'No, dear,' said the little old lady firmly. Denise shrugged and looked at Annie. 'Well, boss,' she asked, 'how've we done?'

Annie turned round to look at them – at Denise dressed up to the nines and well into the tens, at Moonpaw putting out paper plates, and at Rainbow cursing away behind the bar, looks of prim satisfaction hovering from their sensible shoes to their freshly hennaed hair.

Annie couldn't resist it. She clapped her hands. 'Oh!' she squeaked. She squeezed her eyes tight. Odd that this was the biggest party she'd ever organised in her life. Not in a million years. But hey – tonight was her night.

'Oh,' she said, 'thank you for making me do this.' She giggled.

Denise laughed too. 'Come on, girls, let's give 'em Bingo! Open the floodgates!'

And they came.

Rainbow and Moonpaw, their shoes squeaking on the flooring, swung the doors open, and in came customer after customer. Annie had told herself, several times, 'If I can just beat eight, then I'm not a failure. Twenty would be lovely. Forty… now that's pretty much Ministry Of Sound.'

They poured in. There was a queue, a queue of people handing over money, nodding and shuffling in. Looking around at the room, and smiling. They bought drinks! They mingled!

Moonpaw tapped her on the arm. 'Lovely work,' she breathed. 'We've a lot of new folks. Well done, girl.'

'I know!' sighed Annie. 'This is brilliant! Oh, thank you.'

'I only hope they know how to play Bingo,' Moonpaw said seriously.

'Who cares?' laughed Annie.

Moonpaw gave her a sharp look. 'It wouldn't be proper, my child,' she said firmly. She glanced protectively at the prize table and tutted.

Denise appeared at Moonpaw's elbow. 'Moonpaw love,

Rainbow's swamped at the bar – can you lend a hand?'

Moonpaw looked up at her, all smiles, 'Righty-ho, my child. Best get over there before she hits someone. All hands to the pumps!' She shuffled off in a jingle of jewellery.

Annie nodded at Denise, and watched her get back to taking money. Denise grinned and talked to the crowd as they came in, sending them off to the bar. And for a second, in among all her success, Annie felt a bit jealous – she wished she could do that. Just fit in. Just be a part. Just mingle.

Then she realised they were running low on fivers and got on with trying to sort out change.

'We – are – late!' puffed George, running across the dark sports field.

'Relax!' Mitchell's saunter kept up easily with George's anxious running.

'If we're late, she will kill us. You know. Deadly vengeance from beyond the grave.'

Mitchell shrugged, and maliciously lit another cigarette. 'It'll be fine, George. Handful of old biddies, pineapple on a stick, currant Club biscuit and the chance to win a *Die Hard* boxset on VHS. It will be boring.'

'That is not the point,' George sounded hurt. 'You really just don't get people do you? This is about Annie's night! This is her thing.'

'With Denise's help,' said Mitchell, striding past him. He breathed in and exhaled deeply. 'What a brilliant evening! Ah the crisp smell of winter!'

'Yes, fine,' snapped George. He suddenly realised that he was running on the spot, backwards, and turned round, jogging to try and catch up with Mitchell. 'With Denise's help. Lovely. Teamwork is what makes *Sesame Street* such a jolly nice place to live. Can we just hurry up, please?'

Mitchell stood his ground, flicking the glowing stub away across the football pitch. 'Better not let the girls down,' he said to himself, and strode after George.

Annie saw them coming, and her smile spread all the way across her face. 'Guys!' she shouted, swinging almost coquettishly on the door. 'Welcome to Bingo!'

Mitchell and George stamped in, Mitchell sweeping a lock of hair out of his eyes and blinking at the light of the room. And the people. The room was crowded. 'Full house, Annie,' he said.

'I know!' Annie gave a little jump. 'Er, it's a fiver.'

'Right.' said Mitchell without turning. 'George? Pay the lady.'

George reached into his pocket. Annie leaned over. 'Each,' she said.

'OK,' muttered George, reaching into his wallet and wondering if he'd got out enough money. Well, probably, but it was going to be a little tight. It all depended on how much they were charging for drinks. At a pinch, so long as he didn't have to buy any big rounds, things should be fine, allowing for about three pounds max for a glass of wine, maybe the same for a tin of beer, although that would be pushing it. It would be fine. So long as Mitchell wasn't in one of his spirits moods – there was no telling what they'd be charging for them, and then it might be blackcurrant and soda for the rest of the night. Oh, it was all so complex. Still.

George looked up. Annie was smiling at him, hand held out patiently. 'Tenner,' she said softly.

'Right,' said George, and handed the money over.

Annie smiled and handed him a couple of pens. 'Dobber,' she said.

'What?'

'It's your pen for marking your numbers,' whispered Annie solemnly. 'Technical term.'

'All right, then!' enthused George. 'Dob Dob Dob!' He stepped over to Mitchell before he could see Annie's smile fall slightly.

'Where's Denise?' asked Mitchell, vaguely.

'Dunno,' said George handing him a pen. 'But here is your dobber!'

'Lovely.' Mitchell's eyes were scanning the room. 'Get me a gin and tonic would you? Better make it a double.'

'Sure,' said George flatly. 'Great.'

He started to make his way over to the bar when Mitchell's hand clamped onto his shoulder like a vice. 'Don't move,' he hissed.

George made to turn but suddenly found himself spun round, in a group hug with an equally surprised Annie.

'Look at the crowd!' hissed Mitchell.

'I know!' laughed Annie. 'There must be over fifty people here. Maybe a hundred! Moonpaw and Rainbow don't know what to do with themselves. This is going to be the best night ever! God that sounds sad, but no. No, I really mean it!'

'Look at the crowd,' hissed Mitchell again.

Annie looked out across the crammed sports hall. There were people everywhere, at the bar, sitting across the tables, edged up against the tables and along the walls of the room. There was a queue four-deep at the bar, behind which the two old ladies were serving with unhurried sweetness.

'There are so many people! I don't think I've been in a

room full of this many people since I died!' breathed Annie. 'Ooh, can a ghost get claustrophobic? Oh, who cares! I feel so alive! Oh guys, thank you – without you, I'd never have pulled something like this off! A room full of so many, so many...' She paused. 'So many pale... skinny... sinister... people... dressed in black...'

Her voice died away and her mouth hung open.

'Oh my God, they're all vampires!'

'Bingo,' said Mitchell.

BINGO CARD

Below is your Bingo card. Feel free to play along. To find
out if you've won, go to page 254.

4	18		32			64		88
	11	26		43	55		76	
6		22			53	66		80

Coming of Age

18

'This hall is full of vampires!' Annie looked around the room in horror. 'What do we do?' she screamed. She turned to Mitchell. 'Who exactly did you give flyers to?' she demanded.

Mitchell was laconic. 'Don't blame me.'

'It wasn't me,' said George quickly. He coughed. 'Shouldn't we evacuate?'

'Why bother?' Mitchell looked round the hall and shrugged. 'Apart from a couple of old biddies and Denise, it looks like all the rest are vampires. It'd be like spilling a jar of hungry wasps.'

Annie nodded. 'Fine, we'll get the humans out, and then we set fire to the sports hall.'

'Agreed. Mitchell, can we borrow your lighter?' asked George.

'Hey!' Mitchell raised a hand in protest. 'Calm down.

Equal rights! Perhaps… you know… they just want to play Bingo.'

'Vampire… Bingo…' George stuttered to a halt.

'There are some top prizes,' Annie considered. 'Including a selection of sausages. They're organic and responsibly farmed.'

'I just don't care,' said George. 'We're going to stop this before it gets—'

There was a boom of feedback like a thunderclap.

'My lords, ladies and gentlemen!' called Denise from the stage. 'Thank you for coming! Let's get cracking. You've got your books, your dobbers and your luck? Lovely jubbly, crack open the bubbly! Let's get the Bingo train rolling. We'll start off playing for a full line shall we? Throw open your books and I'll fire up the Bingomatic.' She reached over and flicked on something that looked like an ancient clock radio. After a brief pause, it flashed up '11'.

'Cracking! Legs 11! What a great place to start!'

As one, the crowd looked down, scanned their books and crossed off the number if they had it.

'— too late,' finished George lamely.

Moonpaw let in two latecomers and quietly handed them pens and books. They sat themselves down at a table at the back. Of all the people in Bristol to be sat together at a table, it would be these two. They stared at each other sourly.

'Right,' said the little man, licking his lips nervously and trying not to stare at his companion's remarkable comb-over. 'Dr McGough, isn't it?'

Dr McGough neatened his tie and smiled, staring at the other man with an expression of utter weariness. 'Yes it is. And you are…?'

'Gavin Foot,' said the man, trying to draw himself up taller and not look uncomfortable.

'Tom Mix – number 6. Snakes alive – it's number 55. Will you still need me?… Why, it's number 64…'

'The intrepid journalist,' said Dr McGough, letting the words hang in the air. He looked the shabby man up and down and almost instantly dismissed him. 'I read with much interest your little story in the local paper about the hospital. Most fascinating.'

'You had been trying to cover up some very serious events in your hospital.' Gavin felt, oddly, instantly on the defensive. As though Dr McGough wasn't even bothered by him.

Dr McGough scrubbed at a spot on his jacket with a fingernail. 'Now, then, let me just pull you up on that,' he said, with a carefully humourless laugh. 'Not me personally.' He leaned forward with a confidential whisper. 'I'm a new appointment, and these things can look so bad in print whereas, as I'm sure you know, in real life, often people are simply trying to make the best of things. A fact so often nobly overlooked by eager pressmen desperate to fill in the space between the car adverts and the erotic phone lines. I've never believed in conspiracies myself. Especially not…' and he paused, 'in the NHS. Dear me, the paperwork, dear man! And the meetings. Why, the PowerPoint slides alone, imagine. And have you met our head of HR? Ghastly woman.' He raised his pitch a little. '"Well, whilst I really admire the ambition of what you've scoped out, what I was wondering was if we could perhaps de-scale this conspiracy slightly without compromising your valuable goals. What are the key markers we're really aiming for here…?" And so on, like so much jam roly-poly. Horrid people. Normally mothers of too many children who haven't had a thought since first getting pregnant. I am speaking…' a severe glance here, '*off* the record, of course, Mr Foot.'

'Gavin,' said Gavin.

'But Foot is such an interesting surname,' pondered Dr McGough. 'I wonder what its origins are? Whereas Gavin. That is a tiny little name. A nothing. You'll forgive me.' He smiled, patting his hair neatly.

'Would you like a drink?' asked Gavin

Dr McGough beamed. 'You're going to ply me with alcohol in the hope of getting an exclusive, I see. Well, you're welcome to try.' He glanced around the bar. 'I suspect they're limited as to single malts, but see what you can magic up.'

Gavin went and got drinks.

Dr McGough folded open his Bingo book and stared at the numbers critically and then over at Denise, watching her with some interest.

'Bang on the drum – 71. Dirty Gertie – oh, it's number 30! And what's that? We have a winner already! Now come up and choose a prize. Will it be the cutlery set? Come on, everyone, a round of applause!'

Gavin set down the drinks and smiled at Dr McGough, who took a sip of the scotch and managed to hide a wince. 'Hmm, not quite Bells, but an interesting blend, nevertheless. A little bit of Islay, a hint of Jura…'

'And mostly paint stripper?' suggested Gavin.

Dr McGough smiled thinly. 'Stop that, or I shall have

to like you, Mr Foot. Now, what brings our local paper's leading investigative reporter to a charity Bingo night? Surely they've not demoted you to car boot sales and weddings? Oh dear, that would be lachrymose.'

Gavin stopped, halfway through raising his pint. 'I'm not sure that's quite the right word.' He shook his head. 'We're just short-handed. Gone are the days when a newspaper was a room full of bright young things. Now it's pretty much me and a dog on a string. It's good to cover stuff like this – bit of charity, community spirit, and we got a visit from…' He gestured to Denise. 'Photogenic, isn't she?'

Dr McGough considered. 'It would be impolitic of me to comment,' he said. 'She is a patient of mine.'

'Ah,' said Gavin.

'She handed me a flyer and along I came,' Dr McGough spread out his hands. 'Not much else to do when *Strictly* isn't on, alas. Still, this place quite reminds me of holidays at Skegness as a youngster. Why, though, you're too young for Skegness aren't you? Probably traipsing the dunes of Ibiza looking for a foam party or some such.'

Gavin looked morosely at his pint. 'Not my scene, either, I'm afraid. Hadn't we better pay attention to the Bingo?'

'Quite right, quite right.' Dr McGough fixed his eyes reluctantly on his Bingo card. 'I hear I could win a microwave. Fancy.' He listened to Denise call out a few numbers and then sighed. 'I'm not doing very well,' he muttered, leaning over and looking at Gavin's. 'Certainly not as well as you.'

'Do you mind?' said Gavin protectively.

'Oh, come now.' Dr McGough swept a hand through his hair. 'It's not like bridge. I was just seeing how close you were to scoring a line.'

Gavin shook his head. 'Again, not my scene. Perhaps you could tell me if it's true that you're planning on putting in a new patient database?'

'What a dull little man you are,' tutted Dr McGough. 'That microwave would be wasted on you.'

Denise sat up on stage, calling numbers.

'Gandhi's tea – number 80. Number 76 – hope she's worth it. Never been kissed, it's sweet 16...'

She looked at the crowd watching her, occasionally marking their papers, and she looked over at Annie. She winked. It was going brilliantly. She shouldn't look so nervous.

Mitchell and George sat playing away at their Bingo.

'But—' began George.

'Relax!' exclaimed Mitchell in an urgent hiss. 'Look around you. The vampires are actually playing the game. They're not tearing each other apart. You've got to take a more complex view of these things. We're not inhuman monsters – we've got passions too. We've got a soul.'

George looked down at his card again. 'Yes, that's all very well, but Bingo?'

Mitchell shrugged. 'What can I say? I'm not responsible for my people.'

My people? George narrowed his eyes. 'Are you feeling all right? It's just that you're acting...'

Mitchell tapped him on the shoulder. 'Am *I* feeling all right?' he was slurring slightly. 'What about you? Relax. Let your hair down. Or check that Annie's OK. Just stop being an arsehole.' He sniggered.

*

132

And that was pretty much how the Bingo night went for the first hour or so. A bit of music, a few rounds. Denise handing out prizes to a selection of thin-looking winners. Nothing very exciting. George got close to a line and was hopefully eyeing up a mini-hamper of jams. Then they moved on to playing for a full house and he lost out to a rather drab-looking woman in crushed velvet.

George tried to concentrate on the game, but was unsettled. All around him were vampires playing Bingo. Even Mitchell. And they seemed… odd. Complacent. Dopey. Drunk almost. Just sitting there, looking up at Denise, reading the numbers off the Bingomatic.

Denise carried on calling out. 'Key to the door – 21… The men with ropes and sticks – it's number 26… Aww, Suffer in eternity, 43…'

Annie stared in horror as her friend called on obliviously.

'Ask yourself – why can she see you? Number 62. What? No winners here? All right then,' Denise pushed the Bingomatic again. 'And… You're no longer alive – 75. We're coming for you – 32.'

Horrified, Annie gasped, but Denise didn't seem to notice. Annie looked around the hall. No one else seemed to realise what was happening. Could a ghost go crazy? No, Annie. You know what's happening. We'll meet again. You don't know where. But we know when.

'Come on, ladies and gentlemen, we must have a winner now? No? What's that – well, remember, life's not fair and neither's Bingo, eh!'

She looked at Annie and she winked.

*

'Well, I must say, Mr Foot, this looks like quite an event,' said Dr McGough drily as he marked a number off on his card. 'However are you going to fit a report of this into a mere 400 words?'

Gavin shrugged. 'Some stories are big, some stories are small. But it's the people that matter.'

'Indeed?' said Dr McGough, glancing around the room. 'Oh, I shouldn't bother with this lot if I were you.'

Gavin gave a long sigh. 'Nice to hear the view of someone from the caring profession. Can I quote you?'

'Over my dead body,' laughed Dr McGough. He went and got himself another drink and came back, grinning happily.

Gavin looked pointedly at his own empty pint glass.

Dr McGough merely smiled. 'I would have got you a drink, Mr Foot, but you are working.'

George, coming out of the loos, turned quickly away as Dr McGough passed, consternation on his face. What was *he* doing here?

He tried explaining his worries to Mitchell, but Mitchell waved him away. 'Look, George, she's Guffy's patient. And, fair enough, you don't like him, so stop worrying – he's in a room full of the undead. If they get peckish, we can set them on him. These things have a way of sorting themselves out. And who knows, we might even get that new microwave.'

'I'd prefer the cutlery set,' said George. 'But that's not the point. I really don't like this.'

Mitchell nudged him on the shoulder. 'You're just saying that because you're you. And because you've not won at a game. And when was the last time that happened? Ever?'

For a moment, George looked as though he was about

to protest. 'Julia and I only played Monopoly the once,' he admitted. 'She said it brought out a nasty side of me.'

'Ha ha,' said Mitchell. 'If only she knew.'

'You're not mingling, Annie.' Denise gave Annie a shove towards the crowd. They were on a break from Bingo. Moonpaw had put on one of the CDs left over from a jumble sale, and people were milling around bemusedly to Steve Brookstein.

'Oh, you know how it is,' said Annie, smiling nervously and holding her drink close to her. 'I'm just shy.'

'Not good enough,' said Denise, crossing her arms. 'You really need to get out there. Tonight is about you, remember. That's why we organised this. Go out! Meet a few people! Break some hearts!'

'Really?' said Annie. 'Tonight's all about me, is it?'

Denise nodded. 'Of course it is.'

'And those Bingo numbers? Some of those calls were very creative.' Annie narrowed her lips.

'What?' said Denise, her eyes wide and innocent. 'I know I've not got them perfect. I'm just saying what comes into my head. Beginner's luck, that's what it is. I seem to be getting away with it. Why, what do you think?'

'Nothing,' said Annie, shaking her head. Perhaps she was imagining it. But of course you're not, Annie. You know we're waiting.

Changing the subject, Annie pointed at the crowd. 'And you're getting on well with everyone.'

'Oh Annie, you know me. I always have a good time. But what about you? This isn't the you I knew. You were never shy. You were always out there. You'd be one of the first on the dance floor, even if you didn't know the moves.'

'Thanks.' Annie pretended to suck on her drink.

'And now… I dunno. Look at you. It's like the people here can't even see you.'

Annie shrugged. 'Maybe I'm used to this. Maybe I like this. We can't all model ourselves on Lindsay Lohan.'

Denise gasped. 'Take that back, or I'll join Facebook and upload those pictures I've got of your old clubbing outfits.'

'You wouldn't!' gasped Annie, and then suddenly realised… 'No, you mustn't!'

'Oh, don't bet on it. I've still got that shot of you in a crop top for whenever I'm worried I look cheap.'

'You must look at it a lot then,' said Annie hotly.

Denise smiled. 'At least I don't take my fashion tips from Bridget Jones.'

'These clothes are comfy!' protested Annie.

Denise narrowed her eyes. 'And what? You have a whole wardrobe full of identical slumber-party outfits?'

'Um…' said Annie.

'Admit it,' laughed Denise. 'I'm fierce.'

'Oh, you are,' echoed Annie, smiling.

'Come on,' said Denise, fumbling in her bag for something. 'Let's give away some sausages.'

They headed back to the stage.

'Hi,' said the teenage girl.

Mitchell turned around and looked at her, his eyes slightly glassy. 'Well helloooo, little girl.'

'Suzie-Anne,' she told him, sweeping her hair back. 'You gave me a flyer, remember? Told me to come along.'

Mitchell laughed. 'So I did! And look at you, Suzie-Anne, what big… eyes you've got.'

George slapped his hand. 'She is jailbait,' he hissed.

Mitchell shrugged. 'She is not. You're not jailbait, are you, Suzie-Anne? How old are you Suzie-woozy?'

'Fifteen,' said Suzie Anne.

'And mature for her age!' enthused Mitchell.

'There's still about 90 years between the two of you!'

'Ignore my sad friend,' said Mitchell. 'He's just been dumped and will probably never have sex again.'

'Gawd,' said Suzie-Anne. She looked at George and narrowed her eyes. 'Do you want me to introduce him to my friend Keely?' she asked Mitchell. 'She'll jump anything.'

Mitchell turned and looked at George, who was shaking his head in horror. He grinned. 'Why not? Give her a call. Let's make an evening of it!'

'OK,' Suzie-Anne nodded and pottered off.

'What are you doing?' demanded George. 'Are you drunk? Are you drunk and mad?'

Mitchell fixed him loosely with his eyes, and smiled that dopey grin. 'I am living a little and watching you spit like a George Forman miracle grill. Good times.'

'Your round, I believe,' said Gavin pointedly.

Dr McGough looked down sadly at their empty glasses. 'But, Mr Foot…' he whispered, 'surely these are on your expenses?'

Gavin shook his head.

'Oh, well, I see,' coughed McGough. 'Then perhaps I should just fight my way through the crowd. Lager, isn't it?'

Gavin shrugged. 'Whatever you can manage.'

Dr McGough stood at the bar. Truthfully, this wasn't something he was used to. McGough had never had bar presence, and it was something of a relief that he'd made enough of a success of his life not to have to demonstrate this failing regularly. He liked expensive places in London with table service, where nice waitresses with low-cut tops would scuttle across and lean over to take his order while smiling at him.

Now he found himself rammed up against a lot of foul-smelling, badly dressed people, jostling unsuccessfully to catch the eyes of a couple of grave-dodging hippies. He waved a £20 note hopefully and managed a lacklustre 'I say!'

Then he noticed her. Three ahead of him in the queue and a little to the left. He goggled, but moved closer. After all, she might just place his order for him. He tapped her on the shoulder, and she spun round.

'Janice?' he said.

Janice Prescott, the hospital's HR director, stared at him. 'Dr McGough!' she said. 'Fancy meeting you here!'

'I know,' he laughed mirthlessly. 'But what about you? I thought you were off sick? Instead you're looking...' He searched for the words that would be complimentary without involving an industrial tribunal.

But the truth was that Janice Prescott looked extraordinary. Whereas his original impressions had been of a slightly dowdy, mildly puffy dyed-blonde with the vacant cunning of a malicious sheep, here instead was a well-dressed, thin, dark-haired beauty. 'My dear,' he said at last. 'Lustrous! Ah ha! That's the word!'

Janice smiled, and her face's naturally snake-like expression showed through. 'You are kind, Dr McGough. Why yes, I suppose I've had something of a makeover. I've lost a lot of weight these last couple of weeks. I've been trying out a new diet. A few lifestyle changes. And I'm feeling a lot better for them. Really positive energy.'

'Oh, I'm pleased – what was it again? Not swine flu?'

Janice smiled again, as though McGough was missing out on a joke. 'Oh no. Just something nasty that's going round. But believe me, I can't wait to get back on the wards and really get my teeth into my work.'

'Oh that's the spirit! It's wonderful to see such an attitude.'

Janice smirked. 'And it's events like this that are so wonderful, don't you think? A real community spirit. Bringing people together.'

'I…' A little lost for words, Dr McGough looked around the room again. 'Well, yes, I suppose so. They're not quite what I'd have called your typical Bristolians, you know. A rum bunch really.'

Janice looked at him again, and that basilisk stare flickered on. 'Is that so, Dr McGough? I think you'll find we're a town full of surprises.'

'Well, I know, my dear. I mean look at you – the very last person I'd imagine at a Bingo night!'

'But I just love this!' said Janice, looking over to the bar staff. 'And I'm just so… There's something in the air. Isn't there? Can't you just taste it?' She breathed out, giggling. 'You know, I really feel like helping the community.' She finally deigned to notice his pointed expression, and her smile faded slightly. 'Forgive me. Would you like a drink, Dr McGough?'

'Oh yes,' said McGough, watching her place her order, while looking sharply at her shoulder. A look of thought crossed his forehead. He tried to imagine Janice going anywhere without her Blackberry, and a folder full of printouts of her emails. But here she was, having fun. Hmm.

Moonpaw and Rainbow turned to each other.

'Rainbow, my love, I know you are enormously busy, but we are almost out of Ready Salted, and there's a run on pork scratchings. I was wondering if you could possibly…?'

'I'm bloody busy myself you know,' said Rainbow tersely, sneaking a look at the crowd in between refilling the optics. 'I'll nip into the stockroom as soon as I get a sodding chance.'

'Oh, believe me, Rainbow, the last thing I wanted to do was make your life more stressful. I was just commenting that Denise and Annie have done a great job.' Moonpaw laughed, clapping her hands together. 'Those girls are such a blessing to us!'

'Eh?' said Rainbow, momentarily confused. She caught sight of Janice and took her order.

'Well, well, well,' said Dr McGough, settling down again. 'Goodness me! It was crowded there. I'm afraid a dear colleague bought me a drink, so I haven't had a chance to get you one. I know you'll forgive me.' He leaned back and took a sip of his whisky, wetting his lips complacently.

Gavin Foot stared levelly at him for a moment, then pushed back his chair, and went to get himself a drink.

Left alone, Dr McGough looked around the room, his expression hardening. After a while, he pulled out his phone, and stared in horror at the screen. There was no signal in the building.

This was very bad news…

Buckle My Shoe

32

'My God, George!' Annie stared in horror at the table, where some schoolgirl was sitting worryingly close to Mitchell. She appeared to be trying to nibble his ear.

'What is going on?' Annie demanded.

'It's not what you think it is,' explained George. 'This is Suzie-Anne,' he continued, by way of introduction, making Suzie-Anne jump. She gave him a *mad-bastard* glance, then inched a little closer to Mitchell.

'Oh really?' said Annie, her hands on her hips. 'Cos it looks like Mitchell is seducing a teenager. Mitchell!' she yelled, but he took no notice, leaning in closer to Suzie-Anne.

'Oh, you're wasting your time with him,' said George, startling Suzie-Anne even more. 'He's been behaving totally oddly all evening. I think he's drunk.' He laughed, and went for a comical shrug, 'Suddenly I'm watching Roman

Polanski on a date. And I nearly got my hands on those sausages.'

Suzie-Anne stared at George like he was a madman.

'I know.' Annie looked sympathetic. 'Did you see the vampire who won the sausages?'

'Doesn't look like the kind to let meat pass her lips, eh?' said George. 'But I bet she'll polish off a few when she gets home.'

Suzie-Anne's mouth hung open, and she shifted uncertainly in her seat.

'But what's happening here?' Annie shook her hair and pointed at Suzie-Anne, who was backing away slightly.

'Um,' said George. 'Of course. Suzie-Anne, you can't see... ah, Just talking aloud. I was forgetting... er, Suzie-Anne. That is a lovely, novel name. And it's nice to meet someone like you in a friendly room like this. Just me and you and Mitchell. Who are not going to have underage sex imminently.'

Annie wagged a finger. 'They'd better not,' she said and walked off.

Moonpaw slid the drink across the bar, and Denise sniffed it carefully. 'Ah, Red Bull, rum, crème de menthe and a dash of Baileys. Sweet!' She gasped, tasting the drink, and then using it to swallow a pill.

'What was that for, my sweetheart? Was it one of those Beecham's dancing powders? Why, I remember the days when I was so full of illicit pharmaceuticals I rattled.' She gave off a throaty laugh. 'You know, I genuinely swear I can't remember the Summer of Love, but I still get a Christmas card from one of The Kinks.' She frowned. 'Are you sure you're not looking to jolly the evening up?'

Denise shook her head. 'God, no! This is only Bingo! Indigestion. I'm a martyr to it.'

'Well, you wouldn't rather have a green tea rather than a curdled Baileys?'

Denise smiled. 'Contains friendly bacteria, Moonpaw.' And then she saw someone in the crowd, and her smile faded for an instant.

Dr McGough looked up from his mobile to see Gavin looking curiously at him.

'Something up?' asked Gavin.

'Not at all,' chuckled McGough, all radiant smiles. 'My work is never done. Always on call, so to speak. I keep trying to get a signal out, but we appear to be in a blackspot. Pity. I was hoping for news on a patient. Ah well.' A little nervous, he put the phone down, and tried not to glance across at it. 'There's no story for you here, I can assure you.'

Desperately bored, George was now looting a pack of peanuts.

Mitchell was telling Suzie-Anne a long and filthy joke, leaning over the table towards her. Suzie-Anne was listening to it, agog, laughing a little too hard and a bit too loud at each turn in the story.

'And then,' Mitchell was explaining, 'she pulled it out and said, "Is this what you were looking for?" And he said, "Well—"'

'Another minute of this and I am phoning Esther Rantzen,' muttered George. 'You're a creepy old man.'

'Mitchell's younger than you,' snapped Suzie-Anne, giving him a sour glance before turning back to Mitchell. 'And then what?' she demanded.

'Oh, please, just die,' said George under his breath.

Over Suzie-Anne's shoulder, he watched Denise cross the room and start talking to Dr McGough. There was a tenseness to her pose he'd never seen before. He remembered their conversation on the bridge, and he wondered – how many patients did McGough have? Was it entirely usual for a man like that to even have patients? And there he was talking to that journalist… Gavin Foot. Were they somehow in league? Highly unlikely surely?

He looked round the table again, at everyone ignoring him, at Denise talking to that doctor and the miserable-looking journalist, at Annie alone and distant, at the room full of vampires, and he thought, *Life's not fair, and neither's Bingo.*

Unlucky for Some

13

The world ended when Denise pushed the button on the Bingomatic. It was almost like a bomb went off.

She'd been calling off the numbers – an improbable string of doubles – Legs 11, Two fat ladies, two ducks in a row, and then '66' had flashed up, and then another '6'. Denise had blinked.

Annie had seen it. And she'd worried.

As Denise reached forward again, she faltered a little. There was a tiny bit of sweat on her forehead, and she wiped it away. She looked up at the lights, and then at the red numbers on the Bingomatic swimming before her. And then she pressed the button.

George grabbed Suzie-Anne at lightning speed as Mitchell lunged at her, teeth bared.

Suzie-Anne wasn't even beginning to scream when

Mitchell attacked again, throwing George out of the way in an effort to get to the girl.

George's head smashed into a radiator, and he struggled to rise, the room whirling around him.

He watched Suzie-Anne backing away, Mitchell advancing on her, eyes flashing darkly. He saw Suzie-Anne desperately smack a chair down on Mitchell's head, and he tried to get up, to stop Mitchell going for her again.

And George realised it was happening all over the room.

Tables were flipped over, chairs scattered as every vampire in the hall suddenly stood up, heads swinging around the room in search of food.

Annie stood there, watching aghast. It was like *Meerkat Manor*, only not cute, all those heads sweeping from left to right, those cold black eyes, those noses sniffing the air. 'I'm the only person here that's safe,' she thought, and didn't feel comforted by it. She ran to Denise's side. She was still staggering, her hair hanging limp around her.

'Are you all right?' asked Annie.

'No!' snapped Denise. 'God, I feel like crap. Utter crap. What's going on?' She turned her face up, and her pupils were dilated. 'I can't quite… see… what's going on…?' The sweat was on her face like condensation.

Annie felt her. 'You're burning up,' she said.

'And you're so cold,' said Denise, slurring slightly. 'Sorry, no, sorry, I just don't… can you call the next few numbers… I just need to… shut up for a minute…'

'It's honestly not a problem,' said Annie. 'Really. Just come with me – we'll take five in the storeroom.' She led her from the stage.

As Denise moved, several dozen heads followed her every move.

'What about my drink?' asked Denise.

'No.' said Annie firmly. 'We need to go quickly.' She yelled at George for help.

'What?' said Gavin Foot. He was staring in utter bemusement at the room, at the people stood around, their heads swaying and sniffing. 'What is this?'

Dr McGough just sat there, rigid. 'Oh...' he said. 'Oh God.'

'What's happening?' said Gavin. 'What's going on, Dr McGough?'

McGough drained his drink. 'I think,' he said carefully, 'under the circumstances, you should call me Declan.'

Gavin made to get up, but Dr McGough stopped him with an iron grip on his wrist. 'Don't bloody move, Foot. Not an inch. It will keep us alive for a few seconds more while I try and work out what to do.'

'Alive?' gasped Gavin.

'Oh yes,' replied McGough, gravely. 'We're totally buggered.'

One second, Moonpaw and Rainbow were stood behind the bar, facing a mass of people all jostling for drinks; the next, everyone had fallen silent, snapped from a crowd into a wall of blank faces with strange dead eyes.

'Moon...' began Rainbow. 'What the bloody what...?'

'I don't know!' shouted Moonpaw. 'But I'm getting a really bad vibe from it.'

Behind the wall of people staring at them, they could both hear furniture smashing.

'Oh arses,' sighed Rainbow. 'And it was all going so well.'

For a few seconds, there was a strange calm. The glitter ball still spun, casting sparkles and shadows over the dark faces that swept the room in unison. Only the loud hiss and hum from the open microphone and the odd, furtive scuffle of shoe on polished old floorboard broke the silence.

Mitchell staggered to his feet, and supported himself on the plastic chair. 'Thanks,' he said to Suzie-Anne. 'I really needed that. Sorry.'

He could see Denise being dragged off the stage by George and Annie. He could see Gavin, what looked like Dr McGough, and the two little old ladies by the bar. Rubbing the back of his head where Suzie-Anne had hit him, he spoke to the room, his voice low but urgent.

'I don't know how many of you can hear me but you are all in danger. Explanations later, I promise,' he said, his soft voice carrying. 'We… They're disoriented by the smell.' He closed his eyes for a second. It was so strong. Almost overwhelming. Like a really ripe fruit. He opened his eyes with an effort. 'They're adjusting and then they'll start hunting again. OK?'

No reply came, but he could just about hear Suzie-Anne crying quietly.

Mitchell looked around him. 'I think they're blocking the front door. Is there another exit?'

'No,' came Moonpaw's voice from behind the bar.

'Right. Any other rooms?'

'The lavs, and there's a tiny stockroom behind the bar.' This time it was Rainbow's voice, a frightened catch in it.

'Right,' said Mitchell. 'Then everyone who isn't... affected, I suggest you run for whichever's closest.'

They ran. Some to the loos on the left, and some sliding behind the bar, weaving and dodging around those eerily still, eerily silent figures, their heads turning quietly from left to right.

As they ran, the noise started up behind them, a low-down, growling snarling howl. A noise that said, very, very simply and plainly: HUNGRY.

Suzie-Anne and Gavin ran for the front door, Gavin trying not to look at the strange, swaying crowd all around him, their heads nodding. The whole spectacle was macabre in the extreme. Gavin was aware of hands lashing out in his direction, but kept his eyes on the doors. On freedom. He'd heard the warnings to stay away from the door, but he didn't fancy being holed up in a toilet without being able to call the emergency services. His main need was to get away.

A figure staggered in front of him. In normal life, it would have been an ordinary man: about Gavin's height, about his build, wearing a pullover and corduroy trousers.

This was not normal life. The man's face was remarkable. The eyes were solid black – like rocks – and the mouth was hanging open, stretched out like a yawning cat's, displaying rows of pointed, sharp, vicious teeth. The face was swinging towards him, the man's feet lurching, and Gavin ducked around it and out into freedom, bolting out into the night.

He didn't look behind him.

The stockroom was tiny, but somehow Denise, George and

Moonpaw crammed in, Moonpaw slamming the lock in the door home after them.

She sat down on a crate of empty bottles, rolled up the sleeves on her oversized jacket in a practical fashion, and surveyed the room. 'Well, my children,' she said, looking around the tiny room full of people and crisp boxes. 'Does anyone know what's going on?' She could see Denise, slumped on a canvas chair, her head between her knees, with Annie watching over her and an equally worried George. 'If no one has any practical suggestions, perhaps we should call the fuzz...?'

In a bathroom, Dr McGough stared in horror as Rainbow dragged Mitchell in. 'You can't bring that thing in here!' he protested.

'Thanks,' said Mitchell, focusing on him with difficulty.

Behind them something gave a loud roar.

'Too bloody late, ducks,' said Rainbow and slammed the door shut, bolting it. Unsupported, Mitchell slumped to the floor in a daze and stayed down.

McGough tapped his mobile phone, sadly.

'So?' demanded Rainbow, her voice like wire. 'The pigs are on the way?'

'I don't think we can expect police assistance,' he said smoothly. 'Something of a reception blackspot.'

'Well, I wouldn't know,' said Rainbow. 'I'm pay as you go, myself, and I always leave the sodding thing at home.'

'What a pity,' sighed McGough. 'At the very least a game of Snake would have passed the time in the ladies' loos.' He nudged the dazed shape at his feet. 'And what,' he asked sourly, 'are we going to do with this?' He indicated Mitchell's immobile form, blood trickling from his forehead, the dented imprint of someone's shoe still clearly visible.

Rainbow indicated the door. 'I'm more worried about how long that buggering door will hold. Should the crowd turn nasty.'

'*Should the crowd turn nasty,*' repeated McGough with dry amusement.

Outside, someone started to scream very loudly.

Suzie-Anne stood in the corridor, beating on the locked door to the Ladies.

'Oi!' she screamed. 'Let me in!' She beat on the door some more.

Rainbow looked at Dr McGough. 'What the hell's going on?' she asked. 'Shouldn't we let the poor girl in?'

'No,' said McGough, blocking her way smoothly. 'Really best not.'

Rainbow glared at him. 'What do you mean?'

'We've locked that door,' McGough said, 'and it stays locked.'

Denise looked up, her head spinning. 'What's that noise?'

'It's a girl shouting,' said Moonpaw.

'Oh no,' said George.

'Hold on a second,' said Annie, moving towards some cartons of pickled onions and a pile of punctured footballs at the back of the storeroom. 'I'll just see if there's a window or something at the back.' She vanished into the shadows.

Suzie-Anne stood there, screaming until she was hoarse, and still beating on the door. Then she felt a hand on her shoulder and turned around.

'Hello,' said Janice from HR. And she bared her teeth. Behind her, the rest of the vampires also snarled with their fangs.

'What the hell do you think you're doing?' shouted Suzie-Anne, fury mixing with fear. 'Don't you dare lay one finger on me, or I'll have the social on you, I swear. I've done it before. Just you ask Mr Hopkins. They won't let him teach no more.'

Janice tilted her head to one side and stroked Suzie-Anne's shoulder.

'Now then,' she said, speaking carefully and softly. 'Let me just bring you up to speed. The situation here is very simple and it's important that you're appraised of the clear through-line that we're proposing to take before we start picking the low-hanging fruit. Now, I hope I've got your attention. Feel free at any point to raise any issues that you may have. OK?'

Suzie-Anne nodded.

'What you don't understand,' Janice said firmly, 'is that What You Want is not on the table. I don't care. None of us do. We're here for the Taint. It has made us hungry. So hungry. And we just have to feed.'

'Feed!' roared the crowd behind her.

'At the end of the day, what it all boils down to, is that we are simply going to eat you,' said Janice.

And they lunged.

Annie materialised at the back of the hall in time to see the creatures reach Suzie Anne.

The girl started to scream, pointing at the door behind her and wailing, 'Take them! Not me! Take them!'

Janice whipped out a hand, ripping back Suzie-Anne's

hair, and sinking teeth into her neck. The nearest vampires clustered round, bearing her up like a coffin, hoisted flat over the crowd, her arms and legs struggling and flailing, her torso thrashing as rows and rows of teeth bit into her, from her ankles to her wrists, fastening on her neck, on the flesh around her crop top, feeding and feeding.

Suzie-Anne's screams rose, louder and louder until a teenage vampire turned her head around slightly and fastened his mouth over hers, sinking teeth into her lips.

She struggled and struggled, her eyes wide but the noise muffled.

In the storeroom, Moonpaw and George listened. Denise slumped sideways in a chair.

In the toilets, Rainbow and Dr McGough listened. Mitchell slept on the bathroom floor.

And at the back of the Bingo hall, Annie shut her eyes as the vampires fed.

At the gothic castle, it was night. A wonderful night, the stars twinkling in the sky. It was the Banquet of Ghosts. On the long-abandoned driveway, green flames lit the way for spectral carriages drawn by translucent chargers. As each carriage pulled up, undead footmen opened its door, offering a hand down to the extravagantly arrayed figure within, mostly visible against the clear night sky as it stepped neatly up the steps and through the majestic hallway and into the ballroom, a vast space lit by hundreds of black candles.

An orchestra of skeletons played tunes for the flickering shadows that night, shadows that danced majestically around the cracked tiles of the floor, the hems of their skirts failing to stir up the mounds of dust. Mice and rats still ran amongst their glowing ankles and transparent boots, as the waltz sawed and echoed across the hall.

Over there was the ghost of Lady Jane Grey talking to Lord Byron's phantom, dressed as a monk. At the buffet of skulls was the figure of a lady with a crown of snakes in her hair being chatted up by a man in a black suit with darkness spilling from his laughing eyes.

And dancing neatly across the floor a veiled woman pirouetted eternally around a naked youth, his chest punctured with fresh wounds that did not bleed, his face impassively watching as he twirled her round and round.

Sinister old ladies lined the walls, their faces drawn into sneers, just watching the dance with baleful, jealous eyes and pointedly ignoring the advances of politely bowing suits of armour.

The ghosts poured into the room, the ghosts of kings and queens, of murderers and victims, of the famous and the interesting across history, of mothers and children. And as the figures swept into the room, their names were announced by a stately butler, his head tucked underneath his arm.

It was a marvellous, wonderful night, the Banquet of Ghosts. A night of joys and wonders, of black magic and white silk, a night of secrets, for the gossip of ghosts is famously unrepeatable.

It was Annie's turn to be announced. She stepped sheepishly into the lights of the grand staircase, looking at her clothes, transformed into a fluttering wedding gown. She smiled a golden smile and took a stately step forward as the voice of the butler said in magnificently plummy tones: 'Miss Annie—'

Annie snapped out of her daydream. She was standing at the back of a tiny store-cupboard surrounded by crisps and pickles.

'What did you see?' asked George, looking up glumly.

'She's… They killed her…' said Annie, helplessly. 'I couldn't do anything. Nothing.' She stared helplessly at her hands.

'They killed her?' repeated George

'Oh, the poor child!' exclaimed Moonpaw, gripping George's hand.

'What is it out there?' demanded Denise. 'Some kind of gang of Satanists?'

'Oh no, dear,' said Moonpaw, patiently. 'I knew some very nice Satanists once. They wouldn't harm a fly. Different story with chickens, mind.'

'Shut up,' said George sharply.

'Anger is a refuge of the impotent,' said Moonpaw, smiling complacently.

'Shut up, please,' he repeated, more softly.

Denise lifted her head up and looked to the door. Her face caught the light, and it looked dreadful, ringed in sweat. 'I'm not feeling very well. Sorry. Not the most important thing at a time like this.'

George glanced at her, worried.

'You should just sit back,' offered Moonpaw, taking off her jacket.

Denise slipped back in the chair.

Annie leant over her and smoothed out her hair. 'What's wrong with you?' she asked.

'Was it that pill thing, dear?' said Rainbow

'What pill?' asked Annie.

Denise just blinked, her teeth gritted. 'Not feeling so good now…'

George looked back at the door, worried.

'What about that girl?' Rainbow was listening at the door.

'Is she all right, do you think?' she asked.

Dr McGough's hand landed softly on her shoulder. 'I know how hard this must sound, but we must fear the worst.' Surprisingly gently, he led her to a toilet, folded the seat down, and rested her on it. His voice was serious and low. 'I'm afraid we're in a very bad situation. Very bad indeed. We've not seen the worst of it, either. But I'm going to try my best to get us out of this.'

He squeezed Rainbow's hand, then stood up, looking around the tiny bathroom, at the dripping taps, at the three toilets and the breezeblocks with the tiny windows. 'Do you know, this is the first time in my life I've ever been in the Ladies? It feels rather wonderfully wrong.' He smiled. 'Although I had almost expected pot plants and a fitted carpet. Still, another of life's mysteries is solved. There we go.' He looked back at the startled woman in front of him. 'What's your name?' he asked.

'Rainbow Jones,' she said.

McGough arched an eyebrow. 'Really? Well, Rainbow, my name is Declan. And I am about to tell you the grim Truth. We are trapped in a hall full of vampires. Yes. Vampires. You know – blood-sucking creatures of the night. And yes, they are crazy with hunger and will drain our blood. Plus we cannot contact the emergency services, and there is no escape.'

'Bugger,' said Rainbow.

She was locked up in a tiny orange room with the store detective. He was leaning against the desk while she was sat in an ancient plastic chair.

'You're really bad at this,' he said softly. He looked kindly and tired.

She nodded, tightly, and smiled at him weakly. How many times had he had to have this conversation, she wondered?

'I mean, really, toddlers nick sweets better than you.' He smiled.

She put it together – the rings round the eyes, the weariness. Young dad. Well, there we are, Denise, arrested by a DILF. She realised she'd missed a few words.

'… why?' he finished.

She looked at him. 'I fancied some nice shampoo,' she said. 'Staying in a Travelodge.'

'Ah,' he said, and nodded. There was a pause. 'I know what it is, you see. It's not just desperate single mothers. We also get yummy mummies, we get sweet old pensioners, even the odd sticky-fingered vicar. And there's always a reason. Whatever… there's always something. Normally embarrassment.'

She shook her head. 'Not got anything to lose,' she said. 'And I really mean it. Figured I should try something new.'

He laughed. 'You're not very good at it.'

She laughed too. 'No. No, I'm not. But you know… try everything once.' She looked him straight in the eyes and grinned.

'Even staying in a Travelodge?' He was smiling. She noticed he was slightly hiding the wedding ring on his hand.

'Yeah,' she said, smiling back. 'Even that.'

'I'm not calling the police,' he said. 'Just so you know.'

'Thanks,' she said. 'And I guess I don't get to keep the shampoo?'

He shook his head. 'Don't try this again,' he said, and looked away.

She stood up. 'No. As I said, try everything once.' She kissed him lightly on the cheek and told him her room number.

*

Denise came to with a start. She felt the chemicals rushing through her bloodstream. Getting caught for shoplifting... Had that really been just a couple of weeks ago? It felt like a lifetime. Ho. Ho. Ho.

Mitchell dozed. He could hear voices but couldn't move. His head pounded and he felt dizzy. There was something... the hunger, the hunger he'd learnt to ignore, the urge to feed, everything he'd repressed was boiling up. He was starving.

Yeah, what he'd love when he woke up would be coffee, orange juice, full English, toast, cereal and porridge. No, that wouldn't be enough. He couldn't quite remember. But it was a terrible... terrible...

He fought to wake up. Though he knew that the instant he did, he'd have to eat.

He opened an eye and saw the woman sat in front of him. All he'd have to do would be to reach out and feed on her...

Outside, Gavin Foot couldn't decide quite what to do. He wanted to run, but an instinct told him to stay and watch, see what would happen at the sports hall. His mobile was inside, left behind along with a briefcase and a camera. Funny that. He'd always assumed that in a crisis he'd be like those people who died in plane crashes because they were trying to keep hold of their duty free. But no. He'd left his bag behind. Which he rather regretted now. Along with the idea that he'd just run and left everyone behind.

So Gavin Foot crouched behind a bush outside the sports hall. He was a journalist, and he would report what was going on.

As he watched, something remarkable happened.

Janice stepped away from the drained body of the girl and looked at the room full of vampires. She shook her head slightly, and the drunken hunger abated slightly, and she felt... she felt more like herself. What they needed, she realised with a sharp clarity, what they needed was Leadership. And that was what she had. In spades.

'Well, that meal didn't last long, did it?' she said, swelling. 'I know what you're feeling. We're all feeling the Taint. It's somewhere in this building, and we must feed on it. It's maddening us, it's disorienting us, but we must all pull together if we're to achieve our one big goal.'

There came a hammering on the door outside. Janice nodded. 'I was expecting that. The smell is strong, is it not? Why don't you –' she nodded at a couple of burly vampires next to the doors, 'let our brothers and sisters in. This shall become our hub of excellence! Great stuff.' She rubbed her hands together. 'And I'll concentrate on our next problem – we've got to find the Taint. It's hiding in this building. Once we're all here, then we can begin. Yes? Lovely!'

She smiled her most winning smile as the doors swung wide.

They came. As Gavin watched, they came from all corners of the park. Drawn in by the smell, walking across the floodlit sports ground. Normally vicious, sensible hunters, instead they were stumbling like drunks, powerful but confused, they dragged their way to the tiny sports hall. They came down the hill, from the road, up from town and across the park. They shuffled across the playing field, their bodies casting long shadows in the cold blue light as they streamed into the small building.

Slowly, inexorably, mindlessly, all Bristol's vampires were coming to Bingo night.

STUCK IN THE TREE

53

Annie appeared in the Ladies and took in the scene. There was Mitchell, Rainbow and a man. She leaned over Mitchell, seeing his eyes flutter open and his hand start to reach out for Rainbow.

Annie kicked him quickly in the back, and he turned over, a pained growl on his face. 'What are you doing?' he spat.

Annie stared at him. 'You were about to eat that old woman.'

Mitchell shook his head. 'I know... Sorry. Can't help myself. Suddenly the hunger... the Taint. It's like I've got the munchies. Everything smells so good. I've just got to eat. I could even eat you.'

Unable to see Annie, Rainbow and McGough were staring at Mitchell in horror.

'Oh my cocking god,' wailed Rainbow, leaning against

a sink. 'You weren't bloody kidding about them vampires, were you? He's one of 'em! There's one of those bleeding things in here with us.'

'Well, I did try and tell you,' sighed McGough, clearly unused to not being listened to first time. 'We have to kill it,' he finished solemnly.

'It?' protested Mitchell. 'Hey! Look. I don't know what's wrong with me. Something is making me want to kill... I don't know. I'm sorry... I can't think... straight. Please... Move away from me.'

'Pull. Yourself. Together,' snapped Annie, shaking him.

To McGough and Rainbow it looked like Mitchell was starting to have a fit.

'Let's snap off a pipe,' whispered McGough. 'We may be able to use it as a stake.'

'Righty-ho,' said Rainbow, and the two of them reached under a sink.

'Wait!' snapped Mitchell.

'Waiting,' said Rainbow.

'It's not that simple. Something's happening to me,' protested Mitchell thickly. 'It's like... Can't you smell the blood in the air?'

McGough swore softly. His face was grim.

'God, I'm starving,' whined a vampire.

There were enthusiastic murmurs from others in the crowd. They were swaying with hunger, drooling like savage animals. The sports hall was beginning to smell. Sweat, lust and decay were overlaid on the pungency of the Taint.

Janice steadied herself, wiping the sweat out of her eyes. 'Indeed, yes,' she called.

She was pleased how quickly they'd adopted her as their natural leader. She liked to think that this was a clear sign of her leadership skills shining through, skills honed by several courses, a raft-building exercise on Lake Snowdon and more than one tin of worm stew. Janice Prescott, Queen of Vampires.

She surveyed the crowd, now several dozen in number. Old vampires, young vampires. Some of them classically handsome and arrayed in dark suits, some of them reassuringly plain and homely. Tonight they were her very own army of darkness.

'The Taint!' roared the crowd.

'Ah yes,' she said. 'The Taint.' She indicated the doors. 'It's clearly among the humans in one of these two rooms. Our first goal must be to break those doors down and feed. I recommend our first approach is confrontational.'

'Knock Knock!' sang out a voice.

McGough stiffened. 'Janice, is that you?'

'Yes it is, Dr McGough.'

'You're a vampire?'

'Yes, I am, Dr McGough. And we're going to huff and puff and blow your house down.'

'Well, at least you're putting things simply for once.' McGough was dry.

'It's a very flimsy-looking door. There are a lot of us out here.'

'I'm sure there are, dear woman, but you're forgetting something. Come closer.'

McGough stepped up to the door, fingering something concealed in his shirt.

Rainbow listened in horror as there was a scratching on

the other side of the door, followed by a thumping noise, and then a loud hiss.

'Try harder!' screamed Janice's voice.

There was a muffled protest and then a slightly feebler thump.

'Janice, I am armed with an ancient weapon.' McGough's voice rang out proudly. 'I have God on my side. I am a Church Warden. And I am a practising Mason.'

Janice hissed in annoyance. 'Then we'll just have to try door number 2,' she said.

Inside the stockroom, everyone yelped at the sound of the battering ram.

'They're coming for us!' gasped Denise.

The door leapt off its lock, swinging open to reveal a crowd of salivating vampires, a woman in a business suit at their head.

'Hello sweethearts,' she said. 'We've come to eat you all up!'

'Do something, George!' yelled Annie as the vampires burst into the room.

'Right!' said George, running to the front of the group. 'Hold on...' He was distracted by the woman. 'Don't you work at the hospital? You're Miss Prescott, aren't you? Blimey. And now you're a vampire? ... Right. Great. Anyway.' He grabbed at the Star of David round his neck and waved it at them. 'I do not let you in! I definitely do not let you in!'

Janice swept her hair back. 'Public space,' she said. 'Not going to work. And your faith barrier's just not strong enough by itself. It can hold me back, but there are more of us. Can you hold us all back? Just by yourself? Now, next door is a sodding Mason. That's impressive.' She looked at George contemptuously.

'Then – then just leave them!' he screamed. 'I am asking you to leave them!' He drew himself up, snarling. 'Or... I'll do to you... what I did to Herrick.' He glowered.

Janice sighed, unimpressed. 'Get out of my way, Scrappy-Doo,' she hissed, swatting him to one side. 'You're spoiling the smell of the food.'

As the vampires started to pour through the door, Moonpaw stepped to the front of the group.

She coughed pleasantly and tugged at the lapels of her faded suit.

'Good evening, my children,' she said, smiling sweetly. 'I am a High Priestess of Avalon. That good enough for you?'

Janice stared at her, aghast, and tried to move forward.

Moonpaw smiled a little wider. 'And I once danced naked by moonlight in the sacred circle of Stonehenge. Got arrested for it by a policeman. Even married the sweetheart for a brief time.' She folded her arms. 'So as you can see, we are both of us most sincere in our beliefs. I would suggest you leave us in our sanctuary.'

'But the Taint!' screamed a thuggish-looking vampire with shaven head and tattoos. 'Give us the Taint!'

'Oh, give it up,' sighed Janice. 'It's not going to work.' She ushered her troops away from the room. She glanced over her shoulder. 'You can't keep us out for ever. We will be back.'

'Oh, I'm quite sure of that,' said Moonpaw. 'Close the door after you, there's a blessing.'

Annie crouched over George. 'Get up, hero,' she said, shaking him.

George ran up and slammed the door shut, leaning on

it with his full weight. He was joined by Moonpaw's bulk. She looked around the storeroom.

'Well, my dears,' she said, 'I have no idea what that was about. But it was a close squeak. Does anyone have any idea what's going on? And whatever do they mean by *the Taint*?'

'Faith barrier isn't going to hold them for long,' said Mitchell, wearily. He was alone in a corner, away from McGough.

The doctor turned to him, an eyebrow raised. 'Indeed?'

Mitchell nodded, screwing his eyes shut and shaking his head as if to clear it. 'There's only you. And there are more vampires coming. At some point they'll just be able to batter the door down and take you like sardines from a can.'

'Buggery balls,' said Rainbow, tugging at her worry beads.

Denise looked up. 'What's going on…?' she asked, speaking through gritted teeth.

George leaned over, concerned. 'We're stuck in here. We're safe for the moment. Now what's wrong with you? Please tell me. Are you all right? Your teeth… what's wrong with your teeth? Is it what you… what you told me about?'

'Side effect.' She winced and parted her teeth with effort, whimpering. 'Steroids. Calcium levels. Feels like… teeth exploding. Ohhhhh…'

'Is there anything we can do?' asked Annie. 'And why didn't you tell me you were ill?'

'Not the right time for a row.' Denise shook her head, froth starting to come from her lips. 'Can't speak… Ironic… grinding fillings.' She groaned and curled up into a ball.

Annie turned to George. 'What's wrong with her?' she demanded.

'Ah,' said George. 'I don't really know. But she thinks she's dying. Which is why she told me not to tell you.'

'What?' Annie stared at Denise horrified.

Denise looked at her, apologetic but with tears streaming down her face.

'I…' said George uncertainly. 'I don't know exactly. Some kind of virus she said.'

Denise nodded. 'Sorry,' she said. Her teeth clamped down on her lip and blood oozed from it. She winced with silent pain. She tried to open her mouth, but couldn't.

'We've simply got to do something!' protested Moonpaw.

'Bring down her pulse,' said George quickly. 'She's hyperventilating which isn't going to help… What we need is a nice brown paper bag.' He rummaged around. 'No, plastic bag, kill her in minutes, rubbish George.' Crossly, he kicked over a crate of cans of coke.

'What about this?' asked Moonpaw, handing over something. 'It's my Bag For Life. It's got my knitting in.'

'Perfect!' cried George, scattering the knitting on the floor in a tangle. He threw the woven bag over Denise's head. 'Now,' he said gently, 'breathe deeply and calmly into and out of the bag. In through the nose… out through the mouth… And think… I dunno… calm thoughts.'

Denise sat there, head buried under a bag covered in pastel drawings of root vegetables which wheezed and sagged with her breath.

'Hum,' said Moonpaw, critically. 'It's a sort of first aid, I guess.'

'We need to get her to hospital. All in all it's just one other thing to worry about,' said George. 'We're a little trapped. A lot trapped. There are killers outside. She's ill and we've no way out, and…' He stopped and looked at Annie. 'Where's Mitchell?' he asked.

Outside, Janice slumped down on a bar stool. 'I'm so hungry,' she said. 'Perhaps we should all go out and get a bite to eat?'

'No!' roared an Indian vampire. 'We must have the Taint.' There were roars of agreement.

'Sanjay, isn't it?' Janice smiled wearily. 'I'm always delighted to hear from the minorities, but you've got to be reasonable with me and see things from my point of view. There's a limited supply of food here, but outside is a great big buffet.'

'No!' Sanjay shook his head, and Janice was worried to see how many agreed. 'You're too young to understand.' His face grinned with rapture. 'The Taint is… the sweetest blood. Very rare. So few people have drunk it. And we *want* it.'

'I…' began Janice. For an instant she was worried. Was she losing control? She didn't for an instant think that she was wrong. She was never wrong. But perhaps she should try and see another point of view.

'Breathe it,' urged Sanjay, leaning in. 'Breathe it, please.'

Janice inhaled, deeply. As she did, so did others in the crowd. Every vampire in the hall just stood there, breathing in, smiles spreading across their faces. For an instant, Janice remembered the Bisto adverts. And then the smell from her mother's kitchen of a roast dinner in the oven, with roast potatoes and boiled carrots and peas, and poor Dad whipping up the batter for a Yorkshire pudding and…

She shook her head.

Snap out of it.

Control the beast.

She looked across the hall, crowded with lurching, stumbling, drooling figures. *I'm one of them*, she thought. *I'm nothing better than a beast. An animal.* Janice Prescott had always prided herself on control, on keeping her cool. On a calm smile and an air of quiet superiority. Her best tactic had always been to see off confrontation with a little grin and a meek 'It's OK. You can say it to my face. I can take it.'

And she would. She'd nod, then she'd look personally upset. That little air of victory, of calm, of compassion. Of being better. More mature. More human.

When she'd first found herself a vampire, she'd been quite excited. She was literally superhuman. She was better. Colder, smarter, faster, stronger. She felt as though she'd been recognised for her talents. Given the gift of immortality, because she deserved it.

Also, and she took some pride in this, she enjoyed the killing. It was the sudden answer to that feeling she'd had in meetings. Oh, it was fun enough, ending careers, ruining projects, and just meddling for the sheer giddy hell of it. But it lacked a certain *je ne sais quoi*. How marvellous, she thought, if the sign of a good manager was being able to rip the throats out of people. Second nature.

But here she was, in a Bingo hall, almost against her will. Fighting, fighting to keep her sanity against the ravenous beast within. There was, bubbling underneath her, this vicious awful hunger. A hunger so strong she could smell it. And the blood of that one little girl hadn't gone very far.

'Sanjay, love,' she said. 'I hear what you're saying and I'm going to run something by you. Will you listen to me and tell me what you think, yes?' She looked him right in the eyes and waited until he nodded. 'I've got a compromise solution. It's a question of Human Resources, which is my field of expertise. Why don't you and a couple of the boys nip out and get us some dog-walkers while the rest of us put our heads together and work on the Taint? Surely everyone can see that that will be both brilliant and efficient.' She smiled her widest smile.

McGough knelt down as near to Mitchell as he dared. He passed him a wad of toilet paper, which the vampire used to wipe some of the sweat from his face.

'It's like a fever…' he moaned. 'I feel so drunk. What's happening to me?'

'I can't say,' muttered McGough. 'Tell me. What is your name?'

'Mitchell…' he slurred.

McGough nodded. 'Ah yes. One of the hospital porters, yes? I had no idea we were employing your sort. Goodness me, the undead are everywhere! I knew this would happen when the Poles started going home.' McGough rolled his eyes theatrically. 'You see, my dear Miss Rainbow, that man on the floor is a creature who exists only to feed on the blood of the living. I don't suspect you believe in evolution, do you, my dear, but if you did, then that thing is merely a dead end with good PR and a lot of miserable teenage friends. But to me he's an abomination. And we're currently trapped in here with him.'

'Thanks for the bit about the teenagers,' muttered Mitchell, shaking his head. 'You know what…? I feel so drunk… Absolutely plastered.'

'That'll be this Taint, I think. A fascinating effect. But a drunk vampire is just as lethal as a drunk driver.'

Mitchell's eyes narrowed. 'Do you always speak like that?'

McGough glared at Mitchell. 'How dare you? I spend my life caring for the sick. What do you do? You mop my floors. What a waste of immortality.' He rolled his eyes theatrically.

Mitchell propped himself gingerly on one elbow. 'Motivational speaking not really your strong point, is it?' He sank back down to the floor. 'If I could stand up I would tear your throat out right now.'

Sensing a fight, Rainbow placed herself carefully between the two. 'Calm down, my sweet buggers.' She paused, holding up a palm between Mitchell's rolling gaze and McGough's dry glare. 'I mean it's a lot to take in, isn't it? I came out for Bingo and a bit of bloody quiche, and here I am held hostage by the sodding undead.'

McGough folded his arms and tutted loudly. 'I know, dear lady, I know. It must be shocking for you.' He turned and scowled at Mitchell. 'Shame on you,' he tutted.

Annie materialised back in the storeroom. George looked at her. 'How's it going?' he asked.

'Not good,' she said. 'They're fighting next door.'

'How do you know that, dear?' asked Moonpaw sharply, looking up from Denise.

'If you stand at the back of the room, you can just hear the shouting through the wall,' Annie explained quickly. 'God, they're really going for it. I'm surprised you can't hear it.'

'Can't hear so well at my age,' said Moonpaw. 'Dancing too close to the speakers at the first Glastonbury. Gave away

171

all my money to a maharishi. Never got a single penny back.'

'Not… fever…' Denise said, her teeth clenched, blood starting to leak from her gums. She'd given up on the hemp bag. It wasn't really helping.

'We need to get that child to a hospital,' said Moonpaw firmly.

George held his mobile up, helpless. 'No signal. No police. No ambulance. No fire brigade. Can't even get the coastguard.'

'We did a car boot for the RNLI once,' said Moonpaw wistfully. 'Picked up a lovely set of wheat-sheaf coasters.'

'We've got to think of something,' protested George.

Annie looked at Denise. She was furious with her. Furious that she'd told George but not her. Of all the people to choose. *Since when did we keep secrets from each other?* she felt like shouting. *Mind you, not told her you're a ghost yet, have you, Annie?* That was different. Of course.

'It's getting worse…' whimpered Denise.

Annie leant over her guiltily. 'Yeah, yeah, I know. We'll try and get you out of here.'

'Not likely is it…?' muttered Denise.

'Guess not,' said Annie, and rocked back on her heels. She indicated a crate of vodka. 'What about a drink?'

Denise managed a small smile.

Over the pounding in his ears and the empty hunger clawing at his stomach, Mitchell realised something. His dark gaze hardened slightly and he focused with difficulty on McGough. 'You know a lot about vampires,' he said, trying not to slur his words. His voice sounded very faint and a long way away. 'You know what's going on here. You know what's causing it, you said it was called...'

'The bloody Taint, he said,' put in Rainbow.

'Thank you,' said McGough, drily. 'How appropriate... I suppose there is no use in denying it. I am familiar with vampires. I can recognise one. And I know that what is driving them wild here is a blood fever. It's not unlike what happens in the common flea – another vicious little bloodsucker. If deprived of food, the flea will frantically mate, reproducing in a desperate frenzy, determined that one of its offspring will somehow find a host.'

He smiled, warming to his theory.

'If you shut a handful of fleas in a room and come back in a week or two, you'll find it full of desperately leaping beasties. It's an exaggeration of their natural pattern – like they've changed gear. And that's what's happening with these creatures. You can see the symptoms in Mitchell here. A normal predatory circumspection has been bypassed. These vampires are drunk, drunk on the idea of feeding.'

'How do you know so sodding much about it all?' said Rainbow, suspicious.

McGough sighed. 'I'm simply well informed. Now then, dear lady, Mitchell and I have to talk. This is fascinating. You see, I haven't had a chance to really study the effect on one of my subjects up close.'

'Your subjects?'

Janice's voice boomed out, echoing through the doors of the storeroom and the Ladies. 'Attention human victims! I'm just going to start with a brief précis of the situation at hand. Feel free to shout out if you've any questions that come to mind. But, to briefly run through the bullets – There are two sets of you. We are hungry – And we're going to eat you. This is not a great outcome for you. What I'm going to propose is a bit more even-handed, if not an actual win-win.'

McGough rolled his eyes. 'Dear God, that woman is even worse now she's dead.'

'You are, I hope, familiar with the management training exercise of the Prisoner's Dilemma?' Janice continued. 'I'm going to utilise it as a toolkit to unlock this present scenario. To break it down into practical outcomes…' She breathed. 'You've got five minutes. The first room to send someone out for us to feed on gets to live. We'll set you free and destroy the other room entirely. That's the offer we've got on the table.'

QUEEN BEE

73

'My God,' said George, 'Setting us against each other? That woman's crazy. That's not even human…'

'She's a bitch. A vampire bitch,' said Annie. 'Do you think we can fight our way out? I mean, I don't think I could manage to throw a pencil. I'm useless.' She paused, fondling a packet of Ready Salted. 'Unless… Wait! What if I went out to them? You know, I could go. Offer myself up as a sacrifice.'

'I think they'd see through you quite rapidly. If they can see you at all.'

'Well, they really won't like you,' Annie hissed. George shushed her. *Let's not get overheard.*

'Oh that's right,' he said awkwardly. 'Vampires don't like the taste of me.'

Moonpaw glared at him. 'How do you know that?'

'I… I just do,' said George.

'I see, dear. It's all right for some. Highly convenient, if you don't mind me saying, my child. My first husband was allergic to hard work. Always got a rash when it was time to put up the teepee. That's all I'm saying.'

'Sorry,' George babbled helplessly. 'Please believe me, they wouldn't be interested in me.'

'So,' Moonpaw huffed. 'I take it, young George, that you're waiting for one of us girls to volunteer?'

'No,' said George. 'I mean, well, would you?'

Moonpaw shrugged. '*Taggart* marathon on ITV4 later.' She started rifling through her raffia handbag. 'Probably got some St John's Wort in here. Or at least some Sanatogen.' She gave a little cry and shook a tiny bottle triumphantly. 'This will do nicely! Temazepam! Stun an elephant, that would!'

She leant over Denise. 'All we have to do is prise those choppers apart and we're in business.' She pushed a finger against her teeth without luck. 'I don't suppose anyone's got a screwdriver on them? Or a knife?'

Denise's eyes went wide.

Moonpaw patted her. 'Shhh. Don't panic, dear. Honestly, I've had less trouble worming cats. I just need to get these teeth apart enough to…'

She massaged Denise's lower jaw slightly and managed to squeeze a pill through.

'There we are! Bombs away.' Moonpaw leaned back, satisfied. 'Ah well, with that much sedative inside you, you'll be the calmest one here, ha ha. Probably lead us all to safety. Good-oh.'

Outside the hall, Gavin Foot remained hidden behind a bush, watching. He was cold and the air was icy. It was uncomfortable – he'd settled into a low crouch that had ached into cramp so he was now kneeling, the damp earth soaking up into his knees. He dared not move, no matter how much his legs or, oddly now, his shoulder asked him to. He was fixed to the spot, staring at events played out in the distance, floodlit like some kind of stage show. He watched a small group head out from the sports hall. They stood in the frosty air, sniffing at the breeze. For an instant they stared in his direction, and Gavin froze in horror, suddenly feeling that the bush was invisible. Then, with one movement, their heads swung off to the right, and they marched off, their shadows stretching off across the playing ground like creeping giants.

'Exit stage left,' thought Gavin. For a moment, all was silence and then he heard cries from the darkness and the urgent, angry growling of a dog that choked off. Then the figures returned, dragging several others into the floodlighting. Gavin could see what looked like a man and a woman in tracksuits, and a tiny old man in a camel-hair coat and flat cap, all struggling. Following at the rear, strangely exotic, was a silhouette in a turban with a large dog slung over its shoulder.

The group, some snarling, some screaming, some crying, strode back into the sports hall. The turbaned figure glanced again in his direction, and then the doors drew shut, leaving Gavin alone in the darkness. He waited for a few minutes, and then he ran away.

'Come on, people!' called Janice. 'We've floated a proposal and so far received zero feedback. What is it to be? Who are you going to send out?'

*

In the bathroom, Rainbow, McGough and George turned to stare at each other.

'Well, it ain't gonna bloody be me, sunshine,' announced Rainbow.

McGough smiled at her beatifically. 'No, my dear Rainbow. I didn't for a moment imagine it would be.'

'What's that supposed to mean?'

'Merely that it is people like you, my dear, who don't load the dishwasher, who leave towels on the floor, and who always take the last chocolate biscuit.'

'Oh, I hate that,' said Mitchell. He and McGough smiled at each other.

'What about the sodding vampire?' growled Rainbow.

Mitchell grinned. 'Thank you. But I'm really not on the menu. I'm afraid it's the rest of you they're after.'

McGough shifted his weight uncomfortably from one foot to the other and straightened his tie in the mirror. 'Well, dear lady, I hope you realise that it will not be me. Oh, don't get me wrong – I am not a selfish man,' he said. 'Believe me, I give so much to the community through my work at the hospital. Whereas you'll just be missed by a couple of dozen cats.'

Rainbow eyed him furiously.

'I have always called a spade a spade.' McGough smiled sadly. 'I'm afraid, seen quite objectively, it will have to be you. I'm sure Mitchell would agree with me, if we gave him the vote. Now, then, let's not keep that awful woman waiting.'

'Aren't we forgetting something about the bloody vampire?' said Rainbow, a hint of desperation in her voice. She gestured to Mitchell.

'Well, it's still alive,' growled McGough.

'Actually, I was wondering…' Rainbow pressed on. 'What he's worth to us?'

Mitchell and McGough stared at her.

'I mean… can't we bargain with the bugger?'

'Bargain with this vampire?' McGough was incredulous, cracking out his most unblinking stare.

'Well, yes,' said Rainbow. 'He's one of the devils. Surely that makes him a hostage?'

Mitchell grinned. 'Not really. I'm not much use to them… Hang on…' He pulled himself up onto his elbows and laughed. 'You've got a point. You have to offer me to them.'

'That's very noble, vampire.' McGough was sour.

Mitchell hoisted himself unsteadily up onto his feet. 'It's not exactly noble. It's practical. It'll take them a moment to realise I'm not human. And hey, they'll probably rush you anyway. If they do, there's a chance it'll give everyone else time to escape.'

'What if it doesn't?' asked Rainbow.

'I don't know,' said Mitchell. 'I'm just so hungry I can't think. That's the other problem… I don't know how much longer I can go without eating you.'

McGough laughed, delighted despite the situation. 'And there we have the truth. The best you can hope for from a vampire is that it will try quite hard not to kill you.'

'No,' said Mitchell, shaking his head wearily. 'I've seen enough killing. That's not it. I… please… Don't confuse me…'

Rainbow looked at Mitchell sadly. Despite her revulsion, she felt the urge to pat him on the shoulder. If she could have, she would have made him a strong, sweet cup of tea there and then. But she didn't. She hesitated. As she did so, she noticed something like triumph in Dr McGough's eyes.

'They're going to offer Mitchell to them!' said Annie.

'Who's that, child?' asked Moonpaw.

'Our flatmate. He's in the other room. I can overhear them talking. They're going to open the door.'

'Right, so we know the other team are making a move.' Moonpaw looked decisive as she gathered her shawls around her. 'We should act now. We need to send someone out before they do!'

'We can't!' protested George. 'These people don't play by the rules. They don't keep promises.'

Annie looked at him sourly. 'They're not the only ones,' she muttered.

'We should assume they'll attack us anyway.' George started hunting round the storeroom. 'What we really need is an offensive weapon.'

'Lovely, dear,' muttered Moonpaw. 'Cos that's what we keep in the sports hall. A full anti-zombie kit.' She sighed, a long, tired, bitter sigh. 'What an evening,' she said, and sat down miserably on a box of crisps.

'It's OK,' Annie said gently

Moonpaw stared at her. 'Just you wait till you get old. Wait till you buy a telly and you think *Oh, that'll see me out.* That's really frightening. And the whole idea that this is even happening – well it's not fair. It's just not.'

George patted her on the shoulder. 'Um,' he said, awkwardly. 'There, there.'

'Single, aren't you?' growled Moonpaw.

'Yeah. Recently, yes,' admitted George.

'I can always tell,' said Moonpaw and stood up, brushing down her skirt. 'I'm not ready to die just yet, thank you. My life may be all about *Midsomer Murders*, but it's still a life.' She looked around the storeroom. 'I bet there's something in here that can help us. Let's find a weapon... Against vampires.' She gave a little laugh at herself. 'With any luck I'll be home in time to feed the cat. He'll be missing me, will puss. Poor thing. Well, I tell you, if we get out of this it'll be tuna all round tonight, goodness me yes.' She beamed.

'Give. Me. Strength,' muttered George under his breath.

Moonpaw gave an excited coo and straightened up from a box clutching a packet of crisps. 'What do you think?' she exclaimed. 'Garlic and Herb!'

George groaned.

Outside Janice turned to the vampires assembled around her. Having feasted on a dog-walker, two joggers, and a German Shepherd, they were now gathered round the bar, proceeding to pretty much empty it.

Janice grabbed a packet of crisps. 'Ooh, Garlic and Herb! Lovely.' She opened the packet and offered it round. 'Come on, people! I believe there's enough of us and we're strong enough now to overcome that faith-based problem. They're nearly out of time. Let's get that battering ram ready. And shall we see if we can clear that bar out of the way, everyone? Come on! Team effort.'

She stood back and let people do the work.

McGough's hand paused on the lock of the door. 'Ready?'

Rainbow nodded grimly.

'I'm totally hammered actually.' Giggling, Mitchell dragged himself to his feet and stood there swaying. 'Why is that?'

'I've made a note of your symptoms,' said McGough.

Mitchell focused on him. 'Hold that thought,' he said.

'I'm opening the door,' said McGough. 'Ms Rainbow, if you could, ah, position yourself behind the vampire and deliver a smart shove, I shall remain here behind the door.'

'Out of harm's way?' asked Rainbow sourly.

'Not at all.' McGough patted his hair. 'It will allow me to seal us inside again swiftly. Shall we dance?'

'Wait!' Mitchell held up a finger and focused on it with difficulty. 'Hmm. Just a tic. I am getting a message through from the spirit world…'

Suddenly Annie was standing there in the bathroom, hands folded on hips. 'Are you drunk?'

'Little bit tiddly,' admitted Mitchell, giggling. 'Apparently it's blood fever.'

'Looks like that night you and George tried ouzo.'

Mitchell shrugged. 'A little, I guess. I am so hungry. I really need to feast on some warm fresh blood.' He sniffed, his face clearing. 'And I could totally murder a kebab. Yeah.'

'We haven't really got time for this,' said Annie.

Mitchell shrugged. 'You're a ghost, I'm a vampire. We've plenty of time.' He did something with his feet and collapsed against one of the stalls. 'Whoopsie.'

'Mitchell! There are normal people here, too. They haven't got much time. Denise is really ill. Remember Denise? My friend?'

'Right… the one who fancies George? What happened there?' Mitchell frowned. 'What's wrong with her? I mean, I'm pretty. I've got really… well, not that I've checked in a mirror recently, but you know, there's cheekbones and hair and so on. But she's after George? That hurts.'

'Denise says she's dying. I think she's got other things on her mind right now.'

'Cool, OK.' Mitchell shrugged. 'Right, this is serious.'

'Yes,' said Annie. 'And I've got an idea.'

'The vampire is talking to himself,' said McGough. 'This is a new symptom.'

'I'm not so sure…' said Rainbow, smiling radiantly. 'I think he may be… speaking to someone we can't see.'

McGough rolled his eyes.

Moonpaw had managed to find some bottles of vodka and, much to her surprise, a box of tampons. She was muttering over them happily.

'I've managed to get a message through to the other room,' said Annie, walking back through the shadows.

'Brilliant,' said George.

Moonpaw looked up. 'Did you tap on the pipes, dear? I used to know Morse code. Will that help? Are they digging a tunnel? Are we getting out of here?'

'Not exactly,' admitted Annie. 'How are you feeling, George?' she asked. 'You know… are you feeling… strong? You know… Grrr?' She mimed fangs and claws.

'Truthfully, no,' sighed George. 'I'm feeling a bit… I dunno. Like, you know when my allergies kick in? You know, that thing that's not quite like hay fever but comes on in summer? Well, anyway, it's like that. You know, bit itchy and sniffly actually, and…' He caught Annie's glare and ground to a halt. 'But it's not very important. Not now.'

'Pity,' said Annie, 'We're going to need to fight our way out in a few minutes. Try your best, eh? I've organised us a top-class diversion.'

She walked over to Denise. 'You going to be OK to walk? And by "walk" I sort of mean "run".'

Denise tried to nod. 'Pills...' she said. 'Handbag... Outside.'

'Not to worry,' said Annie. 'That's just one more thing to sort out. Back in a tic.' She wandered back into the shadows.

'Funny, I don't hear her tapping. I wonder how Rainbow is?' said Moonpaw rifling through the box of tampons she was still fascinated by. 'Ah har!' she said, and smiled triumphantly.

In the bathroom, McGough and Rainbow were pressed nervously up against the door. McGough wrinkling his nose at the smell of talcum and Indian Musk. Mitchell was holding himself upright against a hand-dryer that kept bursting into action.

'Hold on,' said Mitchell, cupping a hand to an ear and grinning. 'Message from next door. I'm being told that I need to look out for a small pink handbag. Not top of the list of things to sort out, but there we go.'

'Fine.' McGough stood by the door. 'Aside from your haberdashery orders, are you ready?'

Mitchell tried to look casual and overbalanced slightly. 'As I'll ever be. Once you've been over the top in the First World War, everything else is downhill, really.'

'You've been...?' began Rainbow.

'Shhh,' said Mitchell. 'Please, no interviews.'

Rainbow and McGough stepped back as Mitchell moved towards the door.

Denise stood up, shaking with effort. She was rubbing her

jaw and staring at Moonpaw. 'Cat's still got my tongue, and I think I've swallowed a filling,' she said reproachfully, 'but I'm feeling a bit better.' She shrugged. 'Anyway. I'm going out to them.'

'No!' cried Annie, running to her side.

Denise shook her head and smiled bravely. 'Annie,' she said, stroking her arm. 'Surely you can see that it's better this way? You've got the rest of your life ahead of you. And I'm just realising I don't. So this makes sense.' She stepped forward.

Annie looked desperately at George.

'I don't know what to do,' said George, helplessly. 'I just don't.'

'Come on people, I think it's time that we heard from you.' Janice's voice sounded impatient.

'No,' said George, loudly and bravely. 'Don't move another step.' He took Denise in his arms and lowered her to her chair. And then, trembling slightly, he went and stood in front of the door.

'We know what has to happen, don't we?' he said, quietly. 'Let's get on with it.'

He strode forward.

'I'm afraid I'm going to have to call time on this,' they all heard Janice shout. 'Make your choice, or we're going to have to make an executive decision with a battering ram.'

A door flew open, and a hooded figure emerged.

Intermission

ON DEATH

George

I don't think anyone had meant for me to see my dead aunt. You know how it is – slightly awkward family occasion ends with Auntie Flo going off to make herself a pot of tea, and she dies unnoticed while the rowing goes on in the living room.

I can't remember why I wandered into the kitchen. I probably wanted something. She'd left me playing in the hallway with my cars. Which would be OK, only Auntie Flo's hall carpet really smelled of dog. Well, dog poo, really. It was a thin, thin flowery carpet, some of it covered with a thick polythene runner, but the rest of it, and you can see it, is really smeared with dung, like the dogs have dragged themselves across it, like it's a giant sheet of Andrex. Which is strange, you know, cos of the adverts with those puppies bounding around with a nice, lovely fresh roll of toilet paper exactly the same colour as their fur. Which is all sorts of shades of wrong, if you think about it.

Anyway, the point is, I'm tired of weaving my cars in around crusty old bits of dog turd, so I go off to try and find some food in the kitchen. Even at that age, I'm wise enough to hygiene to know to ask for something in a wrapper. Auntie Flo's one of those women. She's... well, Dad always called her filthy Flo. Said she'd been the same as a child. I can't even remember why we're round there, in her nasty little semi where the living room smells of damp, the hallways of dog, and the kitchen of sour milk.

But anyway, I'd like a Club biscuit. That'd be nice. Or a Penguin – the red wrappers are my favourites, although I've never worked that one out as red isn't actually my favourite colour and the biscuits all taste the same.

Instead, there's Auntie Flo. She's sat down in her chair, her face plastered with a look of quiet surprise. You know, *Oh!* Like she's realised she's forgotten to set the video, rather than seen the gates of the afterlife. She's quietly tipped over the milk jug, and it's dribbling across the table. And she's wet herself, a little stream trickling down the farmhouse-style chair.

I ask her very politely if I can have a biscuit. And she doesn't say 'yes', because she's dead. But then again, she doesn't say 'no'.

So, when my parents finally finish their row and come in, they find me standing, quietly watching Auntie Flo. Because I've suddenly realised what death is. And I'm eating a Club biscuit.

Annie
Now, don't laugh, but really, it wasn't until I started falling

down those stairs that I'd ever really thought I was going to die. I'm not ducking the question, but you know... I've known people who've lost friends and family, then there was Billy The Really Yellow Kid at school who died from leukaemia. (Got straight As at GCSE which seemed a bit of a cruel irony.) But you know, I never ever really thought about dying.

Sometimes I'd see my parents, and I'd think *I don't want you to die*. I'd feel the same about my grandparents. But, you know... never about me.

The nearest I'd ever got to thinking about death, genuinely, was on roller-coasters. That thing of spinning round and round and upside down and thinking, *Well, yes, I know it's done this for days and days and years without incident, and while I've been queuing for it I've seen it go round five times, but that's not stopping me from worrying about a bolt coming loose, I mean you read about it in the paper, and it could always be you, and it's not really going to drop like this, is it? Ohhhhhhh!* And yeah, I'd scream like a girl, but I am a girl, thank you very much. And every time we went on one, Owen would buy the picture afterwards. You know? The one they take as you go through the scary bit. There would be Owen, arms above his head, laughing. And there would be me, eyes screwed shut, gob wide open.

It was kind of like that, being pushed down those stairs. I mean, I was surprised and angry. Really. I knew Owen had a temper. A really bad temper. He was the kind of guy who punched walls when he was cross, and, ah, stuff, you know – stupid things like that. I'd already quietly decided we weren't getting a cat in case he kicked it. Shame, really. Actually, I'd still really like a cat, but it'd ignore me in favour of Mitchell and George, if one of them didn't eat it first.

But yeah. When Owen pushed me, there was that look in his eyes. A real look of *I don't care what happens to you*. And it felt, felt just like the start of a roller-coaster – even that same expression on his face, and I felt that anticipation, that sickening, exciting feeling of the world falling away. But also the odd thought that there's no harness this time. I'm not going to get to have a second go at this, am I? And there's no photo this time.

They say your life flashes before you. But why do they say this? Let me tell you, it was just too quick. There was no Greatest Hits. None of that. Just a lot of carpet travelling by very quickly, and Owen standing there getting further away. Like he was at the end of a long, long corridor. And then an odd pain at the back of my head. A pain that I wished would stop. And it did.

Mitchell

No, I did not have a lovely war. Did you see that thing a while back about the last living soldier from the Great War dying? I did. Poor bastard, I thought. For one thing, he's had to live with his memories for as long as I have. For another, he was a fraud without even realising it. For here I am, beating him by a long chalk. Still alive, thank you very much. Been all the way through that war and out the other end.

I'd never seen anyone die before then. It's quite surprising at the start – just the sudden way it takes them. Not neatly, either. One second you're running through a trench, the next you're picking their teeth off your lapel. You're not screaming. You stop doing that quite quickly. And you stop lending people money and fags. You just draw a line and you go *I'm not getting anything back*.

At the start of it, you're with the people you grew up with. The guys you liked and the guys you didn't. All in uniform together, all looking like kids playing soldiers. And all pretending that it's great. And then, after a week or two, you're no longer with them. They've all gone. And it's just you. And you think you're being saved for something greater.

In an odd way, I guess you could say, I was being saved for something else. Just not something greater. But you get a feeling about you. After a while. An idea that you're cheating the odds. That you're winning. And all the time, death is getting closer and closer.

And, actually, if you win, there's no prize. You just get to go home with a whole load of memories that you'd rather not have, a limp, a few scars from razor wire, and the chance to have your old life back. Providing you've not lost too many limbs to make it worthwhile, and that you're hardy enough to survive the influenza outbreak that's sweeping across the globe.

Oddly, that was what made Herrick's offer so tempting. There we were – guns all around us, the dead lying everywhere.

'Look at all this, lad,' he said, his arm sweeping across the desolate woodlands. 'Look at death. Nasty process. In the old days, you'd have a nice little war, get a few knocks and bruises, but, you know, nearly everyone would be home in time for…'

'Christmas?'

'Yes, they really would be. And that would be nice, wouldn't it? Holly, mistletoe, ivy, prize turkeys, puddings, God bless us every one, and so forth.' He flashed me a look of genuine regret. 'But not now. No. Death's just got too efficient for humans. So, what I'm asking you is… Do you want to be something better?'

That was his argument really. Humanity's weakness was death. Time to move on up. Time to be something better.

Herrick waved an arm around the battlefield. It was a short arm. Later I'd wonder if he had his army uniforms taken in. At the time I was just shit scared. That man had such a face – as venomous as it was charming. He turned down the smile just enough to hide the points of his teeth and clapped me on the shoulder. 'Come on, lad,' he said.

'The name's Mitchell,' I said.

'Mitchell. Right.' He nodded, like we were suddenly great friends sharing a confidence. 'It's not great here is it, Mitchell? Come to the future. In our world no one gets left behind.'

Of course, he was right and he was wrong. Actually he was leaving behind everything that being human was all about.

Denise
To be honest, my first meeting with Dr McGough was a bit of a bummer.

'I'm sorry, would you repeat that bit, please?' I said. Well, not those words, exactly.

He blinked a little, fiddled with his tie, and rested himself against his desk. 'My dear,' he said. 'You mean no one's told you?'

He had to repeat that question as well. I guess that's what going into shock's all about. Your brain becomes like some weird CD that's spinning so fast it's skipping tracks all over the place, and I was thinking all sorts of random stuff like *How?* and *Why?* and *Well, at least that answers all sorts of questions like will I meet the right guy, will I have kids, will I really turn into my mother in the end?* I suddenly realised I'd better make a will. And my eyes started to focus on all sorts of stuff – really odd stuff. The books on the shelf behind him. Expensive books. But did he ever look at them? Bet not. And then the paperwork on his desk. And the computer. And the awful view out of his window, a car park where I could just see people coming and going and getting into their cars and driving off. Just living.

I wondered how long I'd been quiet for, and I thought how much my mates would laugh at Speechless Denise. Then I looked back at him, that little professional smile like the guy at the airport about to tell you there'll be a delay, and I was thinking, *This is a 15-minute consultation, right? And he's had to tell me I'm going to die. Is this going to throw out his schedule, or can he get me in and out in under a quarter of an hour?*

'How long have I got to live?' I asked him.

'Ohhh, the biggie! Really?' He shook his head and started to polish his glasses. 'I'm sorry,' he said awkwardly, 'I'm just surprised. You really weren't told this?'

'I found out in Greece,' I explained. 'The doctor didn't speak much English, and my Greek is limited to "Where is the coach?" and "Have you seen the suitcases?" I honestly had no idea.'

'Right.' He hemmed and hummed, and I suddenly realised he didn't do much of the front-line telling-people-they're-dying stuff. He wasn't any good at it. 'Fine. Well, simply put, this is a manageable condition. That's not the same as curable. I'm afraid there is no cure. But we can dramatically slow down the progression. You have an extremely rare virus – a remarkably efficient one.

193

'As of now, it has pretty much taken over your immune system. Think of that as a photocopier, churning out lovely white blood cells that attack any infection. The problem is, this virus has taken over that photocopier, and every time your body has to try and fight off a cold, an infection, or even a hangover, that photocopier now spews out more copies of the virus. The greater the infection, the more desperately that photocopier runs. Your body is destroying itself, I'm afraid, my dear.'

'…' I said.

He leaned forward, just slightly. 'If the process remains unchecked, that is. But there is good news. Thank God for AIDS, I say.'

'I'm sorry?'

'Oh my dear, God Bless It. Thanks to AIDS, we've got so good at understanding how the immune system runs in the last two decades. And the pills that can fiddle with it – oh wondrous! The stuff we can give you… remarkable!'

'So I'm going to live?'

'Well, let's not be hasty.' Dr McGough pulled a thin little smile and patted his ridiculous little hair. 'We're all going to die, my dear. I'm afraid some of us get to realise that unpleasant fact a bit earlier than others. It's a sad irony that you'd actually be in a better situation if you had AIDS. These off-the-shelf combination treatments are very specifically designed to kill off that little bastard. Honestly, one pill a day. Brilliant! But there are a few slightly older treatments that work in isolation – and it's those I'll be working with on you. We've got to try and support your immune system, take back control of that evil photocopier, and eventually work out what to do with all those copies of the virus that are in your system.

'You see, what's fascinating is that what's in your blood isn't something as new and sexy as AIDS. No, my dear, it's very, very old indeed.'

At the time, that didn't make any sense. Only later would I understand that he meant what he said.

GET UP AND RUN

31

With a squeak of sneakers on parquet flooring the hooded figure staggered out of the bathroom and the vampires fell on him.

Janice hissed with anger as the toilet door slammed shut again.

'We have turned them against each other!' she exulted, 'and we have this one to feed on!' She ripped the hood off his head.

'Surprise,' said Mitchell.

Janice stared. 'You!' she screamed.

'Hello!' Mitchell grinned. 'Interesting, isn't it?' he picked at some dirt under a nail. 'Don't I know you? Aren't you... the hospital's Head of HR? Sorry – *weren't* you the hospital's head of HR?'

Janice frowned. 'I see no reason why I can't continue in the post. Firing me would be discrimination.'

'Really?' Mitchell smirked. 'And they're not going to complain when you start eating the patients?'

Janice shrugged. 'We'll cross that bridge when we come to it. As the head of HR, I have always had an exemplary record for accommodating the needs of minorities.'

Mitchell shook his head. 'You're quite a piece of work, Miss Prescott.'

'Thank you.'

'Not a compliment.'

'Doesn't matter. Kill him!' she ordered.

No one moved.

Mitchell smiled. 'You're new to this, aren't you? You don't even know who I am to these people, do you?' His eyes suddenly cleared, and he grinned. He paused, patting Janice on the shoulder. 'I'll bring you up to speed, yes?'

He made his way onto the stage, picked up the microphone and blew into it.

'Ladies and gentlemen—' There was a blast of feedback and Mitchell wobbled a little. 'Right. Er… Good to see some familiar faces here and a few new… comrades. Hey! How's it going? Great.' He paused, a dopey expression spreading across his face. 'Something in the air tonight, isn't there? But let's get to business. I declare this extraordinary meeting of the Vampire Council open!' He nodded to the room. 'We've let things lapse since Mr Herrick… resigned his position. But I think now's a great time to catch up. Shall we crack on? First of all, I'd just like to give you a big hand for coming!'

Mitchell clapped. The vampires clapped back. And, if Mitchell staggered just slightly on his feet, they were too polite to mention it.

'Now then, brethren, if I may,' continued Mitchell. 'Let's—'

'Excuse me.' Janice cut across him. 'If this really is a meeting, shouldn't there be an agenda? And what exactly is the Vampire Council? Is there a working party?'

Mitchell grinned. 'Ah, Miss Prescott. I'm afraid as a new initiate, you're not currently privy to any of the many working parties that make up the Vampire Council. Isn't that right, brothers?'

There was nodding and smiling across the room.

Mitchell continued, 'Of course, if you'd like to put your name forward, then I'm sure it would be… considered. In due time. First off, shall we get back to the Bingo! We've still got a microwave and a cutlery set to win!'

'But!' exclaimed Janice. 'I have natural leadership skills! I'm a born manager! I really must insist…'

Mitchell turned away, appearing to consider this. Then he shrugged. 'OK then. You put your case forward, and we'll listen.'

'But,' gasped Janice, 'I haven't had a chance to prepare. Ideally I'd need time to jot my thoughts down on a few PowerPoints.'

Mitchell shook his head sadly, and then steadied himself. 'No time, Janice. We're vampires. We're dynamic. We're the Can-Do Crowd. We make stuff happen. You're swimming with the big fish now… That is, if you're ready for it?'

'Of course I am,' snapped Janice, climbing onto the stage. 'Starting now?'

'Absolutely,' said Mitchell, turning away as though he might even have been hiding a smile.

'OK.' said Janice. 'Right. Yes. Well, then.' She cleared her throat. 'Perhaps I'd better just start with a personal statement…'

*

Annie flitted back into the room. It was a hive of activity. She nudged George. 'Mitchell's fine,' she said.

'What's he doing?'

'He's playing for time,' Annie explained.

'How's he doing that?' demanded Moonpaw, looking up from unscrewing the cap on a bottle of vodka.

Annie coughed. 'From what I can hear… he's organised a debating society.'

Moonpaw looked at the bottle in her hands and sniffed it. 'This is such a waste,' she said, dropping a tampon into it.

'Naturally,' continued Janice to a crowd that was starting to shuffle just a little, 'I've placed myself at the disposal of a broad spectrum of interactive interfaces, such as moving forward with the hospital's 2.0 outreach user-surfacing programme, a core module of which I really believe can be bolted on root-and-branch to a lot of the work you do…'

Denise stood up gingerly and leant over George and Annie. She seemed properly awake again, for the first time since the Bingo.

'What's going on out there?' she asked.

'OK,' said Annie. 'Big stuff first. Vampires are real.'

'Oh,' said Denise. 'That's pretty big. You sure?'

Annie nodded. 'Mitchell's one of them.'

'Oh,' said Denise. 'That's pretty big, too. You sure?'

'Yes,' said Annie.

'It's just…' Denise paused. 'See, that would explain the hair. I mean, if he can't see himself in a mirror.'

Annie shrugged. 'OK, that was easier than I thought it would be.'

'I'm brilliant,' said Denise, giggling. 'And, let's face it, I'm stuffed full of tranquillisers, and it's been an odd evening. Last thing I knew, we were playing Bingo.'

'And in my work on the waste management sub-committee, I've rolled out many different toolkits for unpacking a real time strategy that…'

'Nearly ready, dear!' called Moonpaw, grabbing another bottle of vodka.

Annie turned round from listening at the door. 'From the sound of things out there, there's no hurry. That woman can really gas on.' She patted Denise's hand.

'You've got cold hands,' said Denise.

'I know,' said Annie. 'Why didn't you tell me?'

'Durr!' Denise gestured around them – at the tiny cramped stockroom, at the locked door, at the pensioner unwrapping tampons, and she poked Annie in the ribs. 'Because I wanted a normal life, silly.'

'Oh,' said Annie. 'Right.'

'Not your fault,' said Denise. 'I guess some people just don't do normal.'

'I'm sorry,' said Annie.

'About the dying?' Denise shrugged. 'It's fine. Really. I'm fine about it. Well, annoyed, but basically… fine. It's a bit like missing a bus, you know. Utterly pissed off at first, and then it's just a lot of waiting about.' She squeezed Annie's hand. 'Still, at least one of us is still up and about, eh?'

'Yeah…' said Annie.

'It's been great seeing you, it really has.'

'Oh yes,' nodded Annie. 'Likewise.'

*

'There! That's me done,' finished Janice with a little smile. 'Any questions?'

A hand shot up. It was Sanjay. 'That's all very well, Miss Prescott, but what is a Vampire Council?'

Janice spun round to face Mitchell, who shrugged disarmingly. 'Ah well, worth a try,' he said and belched.

Intermission

THE LAST THING I KILLED

George

Well, the last thing I killed was an aloe vera plant. I've always wanted green fingers. My mother, very good with plants. Always kept herbs growing in the window sill. Even Julia – she was a window-box kind of person. But me? Never really. Not so much. I remember I even had trouble with growing mustard and cress at school. I remember soaking the paper towel in water and watching the dish every day, thinking it was amazing that we were just being allowed to create life, right there in the classroom. To grow actual food that we could eat.

And one day I came in and all my little stalks had turned brown and keeled over. A little dry patch in a giant field of mustard and cress. I can remember my teacher looking at me sadly. And I felt cheated of the wonders of creation, there and then.

203

It's been downhill ever since. But, you know, I genuinely figured I could probably manage an aloe vera plant. I'd been trying to get one for ages, for the house. Mitchell kept avoiding the issue. You know, sour look and *are you sure you'll not cock your leg against it?* jokes.

Eventually I just went out and got one. They were selling them outside a newsagents and I just bought one.

'Say hello to Vera!' I beamed, setting it down on the kitchen table.

'Don't name it,' warned Mitchell. 'You'll only get attached to it and then really upset when you kill it.'

I watered it, and it was doing very well, thank you.

'What happens next?' I asked. 'Do we harvest it?'

Mitchell shook his head. 'What, dismember poor Vera? No, just buy the moisturiser from Boots. Don't worry – Vera here is free range; those other poor little plants are grown in battery cages and lead short, miserable lives before being sent to the abattoir.' He patted Vera, protectively. It wasn't long after that that I discovered a tiny pot of Baby Bio hidden at the back of the cupboard.

I'm not sure what killed Vera, but I can remember Mitchell looking at me one day accusingly, and sadly taking the withered stump out to the bottom of the garden, pot and all. It was a rainy day, and a bit of me hoped that would bring it back to life. But no. Mitchell gave me a look when he came back in, wiping the mud off his shoes.

'What did you do to it, George?' he asked.

I shrugged.

'You did remember to water it?' his tone was leading.

I nodded. 'Of course. Why is this my fault?'

'What did you water it with?' Mitchell narrowed his eyes. 'Because, as far as I can tell, the soil smelt bad.'

'I don't know what you mean,' I said.

'Did you water it from the tap, or were you just tipping leftovers in there?'

I shook my head. 'Not tea. I didn't pour Annie's tea in there.'

Mitchell considered. 'You didn't perhaps tip away a leftover gin and tonic in there last week, did you?'

I looked at him, instantly guilty. Mitchell scowled. 'Quinine is a poison, George. Still, at least Vera died drunk. She'd have liked that.'

And that's the last thing I killed. Well, apart from a vampire called Herrick, who I tore limb from limb. But I don't want to talk about that.

Dr McGough

Vampires were the reason I came back to Bristol. If you look into my history, you'll see that I haven't smiled in a photograph since the 1970s. Back then, my wife and I had a lovely little townhouse in Clifton with nice views, a garden, and a lovely young daughter.

And then, one day, we found her dead. Just lying there in bed. As far as the coroner was concerned, Jenny had died from a variety of curious, inter-linking symptoms which explained her heart failure. Of course, the coroner was a shifty-looking young man who avoided my eye because we both knew she'd died from exsanguination. There wasn't a drop of blood left in her body, and we both knew it. It wasn't the only death of a child that way over the summer. We'd heard the rumours. Who hadn't?

I wasn't a fool. I've always been a very deeply practical man, but not a sceptic, not by any means. The pastor at my local church was very understanding, professionally sympathetic, and then, when I started to go into details, he was suddenly abrupt. 'Declan,' he said sharply. 'If you'll just allow me to make a suggestion, I'll stop you short there.' He reached for a pad and, flicking through an old notebook, soon found what he was looking for. He started to copy out a telephone number. No name, no details, just a number. 'Please, Declan, I think it would do you a lot of good if you spoke to these people. They're a group who... Well... Your words will not fall on deaf ears. They're fertile ground.' An earnest look. 'And please, please, don't tell me what they say to you. But I do think they'll do you some good.'

I took the number away with me. I was idly curious – was it some bunch of cranks the priest thought I belonged with? Was I being palmed off on the Samaritans or some quiet loony counselling service? I knew, and had little enough patience with, people who claimed to have been possessed by spirits, but I was aware that tiny pockets of the church ran lovely little retreats for those who felt afflicted. Was that what would happen to me? Curled up in a slightly damp rectory taking part in over-serious seminars for a weekend? I hoped not. I just wanted revenge on what had killed my daughter. I wanted to kill them. And I refused to believe that retribution could be at the end of a phone.

But, all the same, I rang the number.

It changed my life. It made me a killer.

Denise

I killed the spider without thinking about it. I was pissed off and having a terrible day. I was supposed to be leading a tour group up to this monastery on top of a hill. You know – nice boat trip across to a tiny island, walk up a steep slope to the monastery, wander around and then down to the beach to catch some rays and enjoy a complimentary seafood slap-up lunch. (I've always hated the phrase 'slap-up', but it's printed there in the brochure. Along with 'get in!' and 'I'll have some of that'. I hate that brochure.)

Of course, the trek up the hill to the monastery isn't compulsory – nearly everyone stays on the beach with bottles of beer. But there are a few who like the culture. It's normally a couple of the sportier boys, one token God-botherer, and, curiously, the red-headed girls. What is it about redheads and culture?

This trek went wrong. We were halfway up, my chit-chat going over like a cup of cold sick, and already one of the red-heads had run out of water. To be fair, it was like walking up an oven. I'd done this trek before, so I was carrying several spare bottles, but the redhead said the water was hot. Of course it was, luv, not carrying a fridge up the hill, was I? So we sat her down in the shade of an olive tree and fanned her a bit, and then we got to make the last hundred metres up the slope. You could already smell the monastery – it was giving off a really strong whiff of donkey dung. They make their own bread there, but I never bought any. The pong put me off.

Anyway, I looked up from making sure that the red-headed girl hadn't fainted totally away and discovered that, oh joy, two of the boys have gone. I tried to remember their names – probably Jonno and Tommo. It was a good guess. They were sexy enough in a lads-on-holiday way, if you could ignore their lobster-coloured skin. But they'd bunked off. I think they just fancied the climb.

'Wait here,' I said to the girls, who all flopped down on the same stone. Three of them pulled out a guidebook, and the other one reached for a *Shopaholic* novel. I figured they'd be fine. The boys had slipped across the sparse scree and climbed down a slope. They'd found a cave.

'Hey, Denise!' one of them (Jonno? Tommo?) said as I caught up with them. 'Look at this! Wahey!'

These aren't really the words you're dying to hear when entering a remote mountain cave with two plumbers from Kettering. But still, worse things have happened at sea. My nan always used to say that. I could never really work out what she meant.

Anyway, I edged into the cave, aware that there was a slope and quite a fall down to the sea.

'Look,' said the other one (frankly, the one who, if you absolutely had to do one, you would). 'The view's great – I bet we can dive straight into the sea from here.'

'Great,' I said. 'I'm telling you now, it's not our responsibility if you do.' Legally covered, I smiled encouragingly.

I looked around the cave. It had all the makings of 'secret passage into the mountain', in the way that caves on beaches always do when you're a kid. Only this one was a hundred metres up a mountainside. I edged in a bit.

That was when I saw the spider. I hate spiders. Especially really big, orange ones. I backed away, and I slipped on the rock, cos I was balancing. As I slipped, my hand reached out and I crushed the spider in my hand.

It didn't start to hurt at once. I was more worried about the bruise on my arse. But then I opened my hand, and there were… bits… of spider in it. Like big spiky hairs. And blood. Quite a bit. It looked nasty.

Tommo and Jonno were really nice. They said they'd help get me up the hill to the monastery. The freckled girls all got a bit squeamish, but Tommo said he'd look after them. Luckily, one of the monks spoke a bit of English and, when I showed him my hand, he suddenly started to take me really seriously. Like how I want to be treated if I ever go into labour. Rushed down a corridor, to a really stark, whitewashed room. I could just hear the sea, and there was light coming in through a thin, arched window.

This old monk came out. Really old, tiny little man. And the guy from the door was with me, and he was talking, and I could only get one word in ten. Like 'wound' and 'ancient'. And I guessed what's Greek for Giant Evil Spider.

The old guy looked at me and at my hand, and he held it up to the light. I could see the little hairs all stuck in like splinters. He gripped my hand, made a sign, and started to lift them out with tweezers.

He muttered something to the young monk, who explained: 'He says, madam, there is a chance the wound is infected. Could be very bad.'

'Hospital bad?'

The young man looked awkward.

The old monk brought out a silver flask and made to sprinkle it on the wound. He grasped my hand and looked at me. The skin around his eyes was as old and brown as wood. He smiled, speaking English to me for the first time. The accent was as thick as *baklava*, but I could make out the words: 'And now we find out,' he said, and poured the liquid onto my hand. It really stung.

'What's that?' I winced. 'Antiseptic?'

The old monk shook his head sadly. 'No. Holy water.'

And I really wished I hadn't killed that spider.

CANDY STORE

74

Mitchell took a swig from a tin of beer. It was warm, but he was really just doing it for effect. He patted the microwave fondly and looked carefully at Janice. 'You know,' he began, 'they say that some people become cruel when they turn into vampires. Everything nice about them just burns away. Maybe it's part of the curse. Even if you don't actually want to feast on people, there's the shame of having to feed off the family pet... But you, Janice. I mean what was there to lose?'

Janice shrugged. 'It's OK. I can take this.' She smiled sweetly. 'I know that you're desperate, and you're playing for time. But we'll still eat your friends in front of you. We're driving forward to a definite goal there. And trust me, darling, you're not looking so good.'

Mitchell smiled, but he knew she was right. The smell in the air... it was like walking past a branch of Lush. Just intoxicating, cloying, sickening, but driving him on. He really, really needed to feed. It was about all he could think of. He forced out a sheepish grin. 'I'm fine, Janice. And please, don't let me hold your slaughter up. Be my guest.'

Janice crossed over to him and hissed into his face. 'Fine. I think we'll start the killing now.'

She snapped her fingers, and a bench crashed into the storeroom door.

Inside, everyone yelped.

'They're coming for us!' Moonpaw cried.

George gripped Denise.

'OK,' he said. 'Let's do this.'

'Again!' yelled Janice, and the battering ram flew into the door. 'Everyone, put your strength into it. We've got to overcome that faith barrier!'

The storeroom door gave way. As it flew open, the people inside ran out.

Denise had never been so scared. After the claustrophobia of the last hour in that tiny room, she was suddenly out into that sports hall, as George and Annie dragged her across the floor, her heels squeaking on the parquet. Everything passed around her in a flash of teeth, of ragged hair, and of black swollen eyes. Swinging around and around her was the light of the glitter ball, still spinning in a curiously stately way.

And something else. A buzzing noise.

Janice rushed forward, fangs bared.

At exactly the same moment, the microwave pinged.

And that was when the explosions began.

First it was the cutlery set that Mitchell had slammed in the microwave.

Then came Moonpaw, running out of the storeroom throwing Molotov cocktails she'd made out of bottles of spirits stuffed with burning tampons.

The roof was the first bit of the building to burst into flame, the flames running up the rafters. They caught amongst the old Christmas decorations, which fluttered down onto the crowd. Baubles shattered, and tinsel dripped in melting streams onto the floor.

Thick, plastic smoke was in the air, and it was almost impossible to see. Denise looked up as the glitter ball fell burning like an asteroid. An alarm went off, melting tinsel rained down as glass baubles blistered and popped and flames ran everywhere. It was dizzying and choking and she shut her eyes for a moment.

There was another shattering bang and then another flaming glass bottle arced through the air, spilling burning fuel across the floor.

'Bugger,' said Janice.

Denise coughed and choked, her eyes watering. There was smoke everywhere and coughing figures, and she could barely breathe, and she had no idea where the door was. All around her was screaming. She watched as a spark landed in a trail of spirits, fire racing along the floor and leaping up curtains.

A burning figure staggered past her. She didn't recognise it.

There was no sign of the door. There was just thick black smoke all around them. She fell heaving against George. 'Let me go!' she cried, but he still marched them on.

213

The smoke settled around them.

Rainbow and Moonpaw stood outside the burning sports hall.

'I'm so glad to see you,' said Moonpaw.

Rainbow laughed. 'We bloody went for it that time, old girl. Your cat will never believe you, will she?'

'No,' laughed Moonpaw.

They stood watching the sports hall.

'There's still some people in there,' said Rainbow, sadly. She held up the key in her hand. 'I'm giving it another minute and then I'm locking them all in.'

'Burn in hell,' cried Moonpaw emphatically. 'Not that I believe in hell, of course.'

In the thick, black confusion Denise felt herself being slung over a shoulder and dragged to a door. She was vaguely aware of a crowd of people coughing and staggering, as monsters suddenly became balls of fire.

Dr McGough ran out next, pursued by a screaming figure that was mostly just claws and teeth.

'Oh no you don't!' exclaimed Moonpaw, hitting it firmly with a hockey stick. 'Back in the oven.' The screaming, burning creature toppled back into the flames.

'Good to see you, you old swine.' Rainbow peered into the conflagration. 'I don't think we should hold the doors much longer.' She looked at McGough. 'Could you see any of the others?'

McGough, doubled over, shook his head. 'Couldn't... see... a thing.'

*

214

Denise felt George buckling under her weight. Then, as she slumped sideways, another figure lunged out of the smoke. She could see the face suddenly, appallingly clearly. The empty black eyes, the sharp teeth.

When she realised it was Mitchell, she screamed.

Suddenly he lifted her up, grabbing her off the exhausted George.

'You've been going round in circles,' he said, his gentle voice carrying over the roaring flames, 'Come on, this way... I think...' And they both dragged Denise on.

Disoriented, heightened senses overwhelmed by the smell of smoke and burning spirits, Janice staggered up against the bar. She knew her health and safety, of course, and dropped quickly to the floor.

Down among the skirting boards, there was still air. She sucked it into her dead lungs. She still wasn't sure if she needed to breathe or not, but it helped clear her head of the mess of signals, of the noise and the smells. And that terrible, raging hunger had even calmed down.

Whatever remained of the human in Janice shifted back into control. All she could see was a mêlée of running legs and in the distance the door. She was aware of the thick palls of smoke and her once coordinated followers milling around like senseless beasts, occasionally bursting into flame.

A charred body fell by her, its hands and feet still drumming helplessly on the floor, the burning hair letting off a foul smell. Janice shook her head. In the distance she could just make out the doors. She was getting out of this. She crawled forward.

*

Sudden, sharp, cold night air and twinkling stars! Denise inhaled gratefully.

'And that's the last of 'em!' she heard Rainbow cry, slamming the doors shut and locking them.

Denise was flung down on a patch of grass. There was a wet thump and her nostrils filled with the smell of wet earth and distant bonfires.

Pressed over her was a concerned Moonpaw. 'How are you, dear child?'

'Felt better,' admitted Denise.

She coughed again, and realised George was stroking her hair. His face was covered in soot.

'Come on,' he said. 'We've got to get you home.' He picked her up again.

Annie stood watching the sports hall burn.

'Well, well, well,' said Dr McGough. 'What an eventful evening.' He glanced around. 'Well, well, well,' he repeated, rubbing his hands nervously. 'Perhaps I'd best be… getting along home, you know.'

Then he realised Mitchell was at his side. 'You're coming with us,' he said, his voice firm. 'Denise needs your help.'

'Oh no,' said McGough sadly.

Mitchell smiled, showing his teeth. 'Oh yes,' he said, and started to drag the doctor away.

Left behind, the two old ladies stood on the deserted football pitch, looking at the smoke belching out of the lonely sports hall and at the starry sky.

The doors started to thump and bulge, as though a great weight was being hurled at them.

Moonpaw shivered. 'It's nearly a full moon,' she said.

Rainbow nodded. 'It's a cold night. Spring gets later every year.'

'I am sorry about the sports hall,' said Annie to them. Moonpaw blinked. It was as though Annie had just appeared. Ah well, probably just the smoke inhalation.

'It's been a bit of a disaster as a fundraiser, I'm afraid,' said Annie sadly.

'Oh, it's all right,' said Moonpaw. 'Rainbow and I talked about it, and we're fully covered under the insurance. What a blessing! This could well be the best night ever – we'll get the money for a whole new centre. And we owe it all to you. Thank you.'

Rainbow shoved her in the ribs. 'You're a ridiculous old bag, you know,' she growled. 'Talking to yourself like that. Too much time alone with that bloody cat. I'm going home to call the fire brigade and laugh at my horoscope. See you tomorrow if you fancy a cuppa.'

She stumped away.

Moonpaw watched her go and then turned to Annie. 'Daft woman, but a sweetheart,' she sighed, fondly. 'It's like she can't see you. It's as though there's something wrong up there.' She tapped her head. 'Which is ironic, really. I'm the one with the brain tumour.'

'Oh,' said Annie. And realised something.

George and Denise reached the edge of the park, George breaking into racking coughs as they started up the slope.

'What's the point of this?' cried Denise. 'Put me down! Can we just rest? There's no one around.'

The street seemed strangely deserted. It was late evening and there weren't even any dog-walkers. It was as though the town had made its excuses and left them to it.

'They'll escape from that sports hall,' gasped George, all but dragging her. 'They will follow us. We've got… to… get… home…' He leaned up against a lamp post. 'When did you get so heavy?' He shook his head and hoisted her forward again. 'Anyway, get home, call you an ambulance.'

'They'll catch up with us easily!' protested Denise. 'I can barely walk.'

'Not if we get to the house… Sanctuary. Vampires can't enter unless invited.'

'Right.' Denise tried to just take this on board. They passed the lights of a local pub. 'What about there?' cried Denise. 'I'm exhausted, and these shoes weren't made for this…'

George shook his head. 'Public. House. Remember? Might as well try hiding in a Cadbury's Creme Egg.'

'Fair enough,' groaned Denise and staggered on. The top of the hill seemed a long way away.

Not far behind them, Mitchell and Dr McGough were pushing their way through the bushes at the edge of the sports ground. McGough was already out of wind and complaining at the thorns scoring his tweed coat.

'Well, Mr Mitchell,' he gasped, pausing to catch his breath. 'As that was my first escape from anything ever, it didn't go too badly.' He cleared his throat. 'All things considered. Looked at in the round. Most dramatic.'

'Be glad to be alive,' snapped Mitchell. 'Most humans only get one brief look at a vampire nest.'

'A vampire nest, eh? How exciting.' The old doctor carefully unpicked some hawthorn from his jacket. His gaze settled on Mitchell, and hardened. 'May I just say, you seem a lot better, young man.'

Mitchell considered this news, and then nodded. 'We'd better get a move on,' he said calmly. 'They'll be making their way out of the sports hall by now.'

'But surely—'

'Vampires are very hard to kill.'

McGough looked nervously behind him, and then sadly up the hill. 'Right,' he said.

'Come on, Guffy, not far to go, old man,' urged Mitchell, looping an arm through the doctor's elbow.

George and Denise sat exhausted on a wall halfway up the hill.

'Sorry,' she said. 'Just had to stop.'

'It's OK,' said George. 'Feeling a bit under the weather myself, actually. Some kind of allergic reaction, I think. I bet it's because I changed fabric softener.'

Denise smiled at him, fondly. 'I was right. You should get out more. Try out new things. Definitely.'

'I think you can say we've tried that.' George looked at her, his breathing still ragged.

She punched him fondly on the shoulder. 'See, we don't need to get drunk to have a good time.'

'Oh, thank God,' said George. 'Finally having an evening out with you sober.'

'And how's it going?' asked Denise.

George straightened up. 'Surprisingly fun actually. Having a really nice time. All things considered.' He smiled at her and there was the tiniest pause before he spoke again. 'Come on then.'

'Yeah,' said Denise, and she leant on his shoulder. 'Back to yours.'

*

The sports hall doors shattered and burst open, spewing out bales of smoke. Janice, her hair smouldering, strode out, followed by about two dozen vampires.

She looked around the deserted sports field, listening out for sirens.

'It's all right,' she said. 'You can get your breath back. And then we'll go and kill them.'

She shook her head. It was as though it was clearing. For the first time in hours she could think straight. Curious.

She sniffed the air and scented her prey.

KNOCK AT THE DOOR

4

They made it to the house, its cracked salmon-pink plaster making it look like a giant cake at the top of the hill. The living room lights were on like a welcome home.

Denise was exhausted from the run up the hill, and George wasn't in a much better state. Mitchell and McGough drew up behind them at the door. The street was empty.

'Quiet night,' said Mitchell, fishing in his pocket.

'Which is lucky when there's a rampaging army of vampires behind us,' said McGough, looking down the hill in alarm.

'Yes, could you hurry?' said George, hopping from one leg to the other while Mitchell jiggled around with the keys. 'I know this isn't top priority,' he gasped, 'but I really, really need a wee.'

Mitchell finally unlocked the door and threw it open with a theatrical gesture. They piled in, with George vanishing upstairs. Mitchell was the last in.

McGough turned to him. 'I invite you in,' he said courteously.

Mitchell stared at him. 'Doesn't work like that. This is my home.' He smiled sweetly, and shut the door behind them.

Annie was already in the kitchen, putting the kettle on.

'Who's that?' asked Dr McGough.

Denise sank down onto a sofa. 'That'll be Annie,' she said. 'She's so practical at a time like this.'

'Right,' said McGough, straining to see who was at work through the fluttering plastic curtain. He leant over her, taking her pulse. 'I'm sorry,' he said. 'This has probably all been quite a shock for you. I know it has for me.' He straightened up and looked at her. 'Miss O Halloran, you have been in the wars. I'm afraid your condition is worsening.' He frowned. 'Now, I bet you've not been able to get to your medication. Very bad, very bad, but we'll patch you up back in hospital soon enough. I'll call an ambulance.' He flashed his most professionally reassuring smile, and smoothly pulled his mobile out of his pocket.

'That bad?' said Denise, alarmed. 'But I haven't—'

'Now, now,' Dr McGough shushed her gravely. 'I think tonight's been quite a strain. But one should never say...' He coughed and patted her on the shoulder.

Mitchell stared at him, alarmed.

George came thumping down the stairs like a 3-year-old.

'Did you wash your hands?' asked Mitchell.

'Yes.' George looked hurt briefly before settling down on a chair with a whoosh. 'What a day, eh?' He laughed, and then caught Denise's eye. 'How are you?' he asked.

She made a brief attempt at looking brave. 'Felt better...' she croaked.

'Well, you look terrible,' said George. 'If you don't mind me saying.'

'Ah ha!' exclaimed McGough, as though noticing him for the first time. 'Mr Sands! Hello!' He waved. 'Fancy seeing you here! It's like a hospital porter's convention. Don't tell me you're a vampire as well? I really should speak to the head of HR, but dear me, it turns out she's a vampire as well! Goodness me, what an evening!' He flashed on a wintry beam. 'The gang's all here, eh? And what a cosy little place. Still this will do until the ambulance turns up. Ah yes. It will do admirably. Now, just sit back and relax, Denise, dear. You've had a nasty attack and it'll take a bit of getting over, and I know how critical it is if you've missed a dose of your medication, but we'll soon sort that out...'

'That's what I was trying to tell you,' said Denise, pulling back her lips. 'George found my handbag on the way out. I haven't missed a dose.'

McGough dropped his phone. 'Oh Christ,' he said.

'OK,' said Denise slowly. 'Not the reaction I was hoping for.'

McGough scrabbled on the floor for his phone, picked it up and backed away.

Annie nudged George in the ribs. 'I think there's trouble.'

'You think?' said George.

Annie nodded significantly and spoke softly. 'He knew about vampires. Find out what's really wrong with Denise.' She caught Denise's eye and smiled reassuringly.

'What's the matter?' asked Denise.

McGough looked at his phone again, then pocketed it

and looked at Denise shiftily. 'Well, well, as I say, all is good. You know, glad to hear it. We should probably, ah...' Hands jammed in pockets he pointed at George.

Mitchell, more like his normal self, lounged against the wall. He was smiling, but it wasn't amused. 'So, Guffy... You know about vampires, yes?'

McGough nodded.

'Unusual, but fair enough.' Mitchell tilted his head to one side, and, just for an instant, sniffed. 'And you're also Denise's doctor? And you just so happened to come along to the sports hall on a night when she got very ill.'

'I am indeed.' McGough looked deeply unhappy about this fact. 'How lucky I happened to be there.'

'Really?' said George.

'There's no limit to what I'll do for the chance to win some potted meat and a wicker basket,' said McGough, airily. 'And also the chance to support one of my patients' convalescence, of course. In the old days we used to make them weave raffia baskets, can you believe?' He glanced around nervously, his gaze settling on Mitchell. 'That ambulance is taking a long time. Look is there any chance we could get out of here quickly? Very quickly?'

'Why?' asked Mitchell.

'Her condition,' explained McGough. 'It really is very serious. Manageable, but serious.'

'But what is she ill with?' pressed George.

'Ah,' McGough's widest beam. 'I'm afraid there are issues of... patient confidentiality.'

'Oh no,' said Denise, standing up. 'Blood poisoning, that's what it is. You see—'

'Nothing to worry about,' McGough hurried on. 'Not contagious. Very rare. Tropical disease. Perfectly manageable. So long as we get the poor girl to a hospital.'

Mitchell shook his head, wearily.

'Blood poisoning?' said George and looked at Denise.

'Blood poisoning,' affirmed Denise.

'Blood poisoning?' Annie repeated slowly.

They all looked at McGough.

'Hum,' he said.

And then George hit him.

Halfway up the hill, Janice paused and smelt the air. 'Oh… it's back. It's glorious!'

She turned back to the vampires following her, an almost evangelical zeal in her eyes. 'The Taint!' she exhaled. 'The smell is back!'

And the creatures following behind her forgot about their burns, their pain, and just gave themselves to the glorious, mindless hunger, their urge to feast on that sweet smell. Sniffing the air like dogs, they hurried up the hill.

'Right,' said George, breathing uneasily, shaking his hand. 'OK. Right.' He wiped his hand across his forehead. 'You see… Dr McGough knows about vampires. He keeps on letting that fact slip.'

McGough stopped nursing his jaw. 'Ah,' he said.

'Which is curious, isn't it?' said George. 'I mean, Annie and I know about vampires because we live with one.'

'Totally normal house apart from that,' insisted Annie quickly.

'But, you know, it's not really the kind of thing a *Daily Mail* reader like the doctor here would know about, is it?'

'*Telegraph*, actually,' said McGough. 'But… you see… vampires have been my special study for a while. A hobby, if you like. And Bristol is famous for being a vampire hot spot.'

'What?' said Denise. 'Sorry, but what? I know I've been away for two years, but really, suddenly everyone but me knows about vampires?'

McGough sighed, 'First vampire on UK shores landed in Bristol. They're homebodies, really. Good place to find them.'

'Yeah,' said Annie. 'But why?'

McGough didn't respond. When George repeated the question, McGough looked up and smiled. But the smile didn't reach his eyes.

'Ah. Well. You see, I'm trying to destroy them.'

Janice Prescott was dead. The barest, most meagre scraps of her humanity remained. The creature that inhabited her body had killed tonight. It had drunk blood. It had fought. It had been set on fire. But still it carried on. The burns that covered its flesh would have hospitalised a human, but Janice Prescott wasn't human any more. Like most natural hunters, vampires have a high pain threshold and heal quickly. If they don't, they die quickly. So, rather than lie down and give in, Janice Prescott just gave herself over entirely to finding the next source of food. She did that using the strongest of hunting instincts. She could smell her next meal on the air, and it smelt amazing.

Dr McGough looked around the room, as though at a group of not particularly bright medical students.

'Am I...' began George, and then squared himself up. 'Am I going to have to hit you again?'

'George!' protested Denise, but only vaguely.

'Fine!' sighed McGough. 'Fine. There is a virus in Denise's bloodstream. It is a very old, very rare infection. It alters the odour of your blood, Denise. Vampires are very sensitive to the bouquet. It acts on them like pheromones – it disrupts their senses and massively increases their urge to feed.'

Denise struggled to sit up. 'What? I'm what?'

George would have lunged, but Mitchell caught his arm with his eyes shut. He looked as though he was concentrating. 'You're the monster, here,' he said softly. 'I know what the Taint is. Every vampire knows the stories of the Taint – the sweetest blood. Addictive. But no one's drunk it for centuries.'

'Ah, well, the secret was lost,' said McGough. 'Or, rather, hidden. On a remote Greek island. By some Monks.'

'Ohhhhh,' said Denise.

'It does not sound like a great way of wiping them out,' said George.

'Indeed, ah yes,' said McGough. 'The point is it increases the urge to feed over any other single impulse. It stops vampires thinking rationally. It intoxicates them, it draws them in like a siren, and it makes them actually quite inefficient at hunting...'

'You've turned me into catnip!' roared Denise.

McGough shrugged. 'Don't be like that – you're a very, very important woman. You could wipe out the biggest threat to the human race. You see, a very sad, very strange man died recently. I've been following him for a while, and I was able to get a sample of his blood. Blood which is poisonous to vampires.' He glanced at Mitchell. 'I believe you met him.'

'Leo...' Mitchell breathed.

'Yes. If I can combine it with a little of Denise's blood, I'll have the perfect weapon: blood which is as irresistible as it is lethal. You vampires are history.'

There was silence. Annie and George glanced at each other. McGough smiled and stared defiantly at Mitchell. He held his gaze, and then blinked, turning away.

Denise narrowed her eyes. 'Yeah, that's all very well, but… If these pills are wiping the virus out of my system, why did you panic when I said I'd not missed a dose?'

'Ah,' said McGough.

George stood up and towered over him. 'Go on,' he said. 'An explanation would be good.'

McGough licked his lips. 'Right,' he said. 'You see… Denise, I've managed to boost your immune system. So your white blood cell count is up. But I'm afraid I haven't yet managed to stop the virus from running riot in your body.'

'That's not the whole truth, is it?' said Denise.

Rattled, McGough shook his head. 'Well…' he said and paused. 'Well…'

'Tell me,' said Denise.

'The pills actually stimulate your body to increase the viral load. It'll make it easier for us to harvest it before you… ah…'

'Die?' asked Denise.

'Ah…' said McGough and went quiet.

George hit him again.

Three late drinkers staggered out of the Shakespeare. They'd been celebrating a small lottery win. Nothing spectacular, but enough for more than a skinful each. They were standing on the street corner trying to work out whose house to go back to for just one more.

It was the gin that killed them. Tim lived on his own, always let them smoke indoors, but only ever had gin. That made for the filthiest hangovers. They were comparing that with the merits of cheap red at Brian's, or hushed conversation in John's tiny front room so-as-not-to-wake-the-baby, when the vampires fell on them. It was too quick for any of them to cry out.

'Would you please stop hitting me?' muttered McGough. 'I'm fairly sure it's a disciplinary offence.'

George stood over him. Denise sat staring at her doctor in horror.

McGough shrugged. 'The immediate problem we have is that you've taken a pill, which will be setting that little photocopier in your body running. Which isn't good news, is it?'

He gave a cold little smirk and indicated Mitchell.

Denise felt a shiver go down her spine.

Mitchell had been quiet. 'Hey! What gives?' he said sleepily. 'Zoned out for a second.'

'Denise is about to drive you mad again,' said George.

'I see,' said Mitchell, giggling a little.

Denise looked at him. 'Sorry,' she said and tried to smile. 'Nothing personal.'

McGough looked at Mitchell. 'It's curious – clearly you've been exposed to smaller doses over a longer period. Slightly weaker effect on you. Pacifying.'

'There is a right time for your work,' said George tightly, 'and this isn't it.'

McGough held up his hands, peaceably. 'True, true, Mr Sands. But fascinating, isn't it – if I could only refine it…'

'You never give up,' Denise laughed, coughing.

Annie stroked her hair. 'Why didn't you tell us you were ill?' she said.

Denise looked at her. 'It was nice not to have to,' she muttered. 'It was nice pretending to be nothing special. You know – to forget that you're interesting and just have a normal life.' She smiled weakly, and her eyelids fluttered and closed.

McGough nodded. 'She'll sleep now,' he said simply. 'You have to see my point of view. Vampires are a disease. You know them quite well, Mr Sands. They're not redeemable creatures.'

'Mitchell's a good vampire,' protested George.

'Thank you,' said Mitchell.

'Oh really? And how often does he kill?'

'… hardly ever…' muttered Mitchell.

'Well, splendid, I think you've made the case quite admirably. Wonderful.'

'No, but…'

'Vampires are a curse on evolution. An insult to life. And I've dedicated myself to destroying them.'

'By killing off someone innocent?' George was furious. 'Is there anything you can do for her?' he said, his tone dark.

McGough carefully plastered his stray hairs onto his head again. 'Well, if we can get her to the hospital there's probably something we can do… something palliative, so to speak.' He looked sheepish.

'Palliative?' queried George. 'So it's too late?'

Annie sat down on the arm of a chair, sinking through it slightly.

McGough shook his head. 'Maybe not. I mean, she was always… her condition was never…' He paused. 'I'm sorry. Genuinely. It wasn't going to be a good prognosis. But the idea is so… enormously…'

Mitchell gripped him by the shoulders. 'There must be something you can do for her now. Please.'

McGough looked at him. 'Well, there's one or two things in my bag, but really, if you can just wait till we get to the hospital…'

'Now,' said Mitchell, and his voice shook slightly. 'Not just for her… but for me. The effect is really quite…' He grabbed the doctor by the collar and leaned in, grinning, letting him see the darkness in his eyes. 'I'm so hungry I could eat George. But you're closer.'

McGough could see the sweat on Mitchell's forehead.

'Please… I'm not entirely in control of myself.' Mitchell turned to Annie and George, and they saw the expression on his face. 'Please, I'm so sorry… I'm so…' He slumped to the floor.

'Of course,' said McGough, 'I could rig up a drip. That coat stand will do admirably. Hit her with a massive dose of antibiotics.' He started rummaging around in his bag.

'Fine,' said George. 'And if she dies, we will kill you.'

'Ah, an incentive scheme. Lovely.' muttered McGough, and bent over his work.

The vampires turned the corner and ranged up outside the house, sniffing the air.

Calm settled over the house. McGough ran the drip through the coat stand and into the sleeping Denise's arm. Annie sat watching from the arm of a chair. George stood, pacing quietly, and Mitchell settled down on the floor, a dopey, drowsy look on his face.

'How are you feeling?' McGough asked him.

'Whuh?' muttered Mitchell, focusing on him with difficulty and then smiling serenely.

'Still high on the scent, I see. Ah well.' McGough tutted and rolled his eyes. 'It's curious. You've built up some slight immunity. Possibly as a result of prolonged exposure. Otherwise… Good heavens.' He looked carefully at the drip. 'Well, no matter, this stuff should flush through soon…' He stood, brushing the dust off his knees. 'There we are. I'm just going to clean up in your kitchen, if I may.' He pottered through.

Annie leaned over Denise. 'She's sleeping pretty soundly,' she said.

'Drugged,' remarked George bitterly.

Mitchell started to giggle.

'Come on, Tinky-Winky,' said Annie, steering him over to the TV cabinet. 'Let's put on one of your films. Honestly, it's like babysitting.' She slid in an old Laurel and Hardy film, and Mitchell's attention briefly wandered to the screen as a large piano drifted slowly up into the air on teetering ropes while a woman pushed a pram underneath.

'All in all,' said George, 'not the kind of day I was expecting.'

'No,' said Annie quietly.

'The Bingo was good, though,' he continued. 'Apart from… you know…'

'The vampires, the slaughter, one of my friends nearly dying, and the arson?'

'Yup.'

'Did you like the quiche?'

'Didn't get much of a chance to try it, I'm afraid,' said George wistfully.

'Pity,' said Annie. 'I'm proud of my pastry.'

They heard the back door closing very, very quietly.

'That'll be Dr McGough doing a runner,' remarked Annie.

George nodded. 'Bastard,' he said gently.

They got up and went to the kitchen door to watch McGough running to the garden fence.

'Oh well,' said George. 'I'd best check on that ambulance.'

Dr McGough was, truth be told, having a really horrible evening. It should have been his evening of triumph, except for his patient starting to die quite quickly. Still, he'd obtained a recent blood sample and had some very good field data. But he'd also just discovered that the street was surrounded by vampires.

He ducked down low, crouching behind an old tin bath full of plants. Hidden here, he hoped he could wait it out. From where he crouched, he could see the shuffling feet and hear their savage snarls. They were like primal beasts. Junkies. All he had to do was wait a little longer. Theoretically, things were pretty much win-win – the virus in Denise's blood would reach a level that would literally start to poison the air, or the vampires would break into the house, feed on her, and drop dead. Either way, his plan was finishing magnificently. So long as the poor girl didn't die before then.

After all, Denise was as good as finished anyway. He had briefly toyed with getting her back to the hospital and seeing if there was something that would stave off the progression of her condition. But frankly, the girl had had a reasonable innings and with the contents of his pocket he'd be able to wipe vampires off the face of the Earth. The greater good.

So McGough lay pressed tightly against an old bathtub full of plants, watching calmly as Janice's vampires walked to their doom.

Mitchell sat cross-legged on the floor, drowsy and smirking at the screen. Laurel and Hardy were experiencing problems with a tap.

There was a sharp knock on the front door.

'Come in!' he said without thinking.

George opened the door and found himself staring at Janice's crazed group of vampires.

'Hell,' he said. 'Not the ambulance.'

They advanced.

'Right!' yelped George. 'You're not allowed in!' He stood back, getting ready to slam the door.

Janice stepped forward. 'But we've already been invited.' Her lips parted in a sneer.

'You idiot!' screamed Annie, kicking Mitchell. 'Stop them, George!'

George threw himself at the front door, slamming it shut.

The noise woke Denise up.

THE LORD IS MY SHEPHERD

23

Denise

I wake up. I'm in a house. Someone else's house. Comfortable, but a bit studenty. You know – cushions and throws and fairy lights. Hi-fi and telly front-and-centre, so you can tell boys live here – but also quite tidy, so I'm guessing at least one woman. Oh yeah, this would have to be a shared house. That would be it – hope the poor cow isn't on her own, trying to keep order in a house full of boys. There's probably a rota of some sort. Yeah, bet there's a rota.

Ow. Something hurts.

The pain's odd. Like it's not really there. But it's quite massive.

Hangover? No. Not really. Hmm.

Oh, there's a cup of tea on the table by me. That's nice. If only I could reach it. But my arm can't quite seem to… come on, arm… no, it's not moving. Wake up, girl. Look around. You've woken up in worse places. Remember that balcony in Mykonos.

There's an old black and white film on the telly. One of those things I've never really seen the point of – you know, thirty-six coppers leap quickly into a van which drives off, tipping them all out, and they get up and run after it, truncheons waving to a frantically tinkling piano. Love that tinkling piano. If my life ever gets a soundtrack, that's what I'd like for it. Plinky Plink Plonk! Plinky Plink Plonk!

My eyes can't really focus on the film. I try frowning but it's not really helping things much. Wonder if I can change the channel. Where's the remote? Bet it's mid-morning by now – must be time for *Loose Women*. Wonder if John Barrowman's on?

My eyes drift across the room. I can't really control them, they're spinning a little – you know that magic rollover vision you get when you go to bed with a skinful? Yeah, like that. Your bed turns into a ship in a storm, and you're clinging on to the side and wondering whether you're going to fall out or throw up.

Actually, yeah, thanks for asking, I do feel a bit sick. Maybe it's going to be one of those hangovers. Lovely. Better scope out the bathroom, or at least a sink. You classy girl, Denise.

And then I see her – she's leaning over me (why haven't I noticed her before?) and she's wearing pyjamas. Probably wondering who the trash is and how to get rid of her before she has to go off to work. Actually… she's really young, great skin, brilliantly curly hair, worried expression. She puts down another cup of tea by the one I've got already. And she smiles – it's a tiny, sad little smile. And I know her! I'm sure I do. Of course, it's –

My eyes drift down and to the left, and there on the floor is a man, sitting cross-legged like a kid. He's a proper 'meet you in the bar on the first night, bang you senseless and then smirk at you as he neatly avoids you for the rest of the holiday' bastard. His hands are sweeping through his hair, and he's staring at me. It's quite disconcerting actually. He's really, really looking at me... hungrily, almost through me. As though he can see my thoughts.

Then there's a banging noise, and my eyes slide right (sickeningly, eurgh!) – and there's a third guy. He's nervous, very nervous – and the panic suits him. He's got a face made for worrying. And he's got his back to the door, spread across it as though it's being beaten down, and he's gripping the frame tightly and he's sweating frantically. He's screaming. And he's looking at me, and he's looking at the guy on the floor, and he's looking at the girl, and then he's looking back at me, and he's screaming at us to help him.

I can't hear his voice, but I can read his lips. 'They're coming! They're coming!' he's crying. And the door is being pushed open behind him, and his fingers are losing their grip on the door frame...

And I can't move. I wish I could help him, but I can't move. And then my eyes spin around the room – at the frantic boy, at the hungry man, at the sad-eyed girl. And then my eyes roll up and settle on the drip feeding into my arm.

And then I remember...

George

All I can feel is a blind panic. Panic is supposed to concentrate the mind and so on, but it's weird suddenly finding yourself playing the little Dutch boy with his finger in a giant vampire dyke. What's worse, my allergies are playing up again. I swear I'm going down with something. It's my allergies. I never really used to have them, but ever since I became a werewolf I've had really sensitive skin. Ironic, at some level. I wonder if it's to do with heightened senses. Maybe that's it – I'm probably allergic to Denise. Which fits my pattern with women, and that's just absolutely great.

I know now is not perhaps the best time, but I'm starting to feel really itchy, and it's annoying and I wonder if I can get Annie to fetch me an anti-histamine. Non-drowsy is probably best. Not that I'm planning on operating machinery or driving a tractor, but I am holding back an army of the undead.

Mitchell's gone. I can see that. No matter how loudly I shout, he's just sitting there with that idiot grin on his face.

Annie is just staring at Denise, who looks as though she's literally fading away. And I can remember where we got that coat stand from, and how we got a discount because it was a little wobbly and we painted it up and now it's part of a field hospital. Funny how evenings go, really.

This was supposed to be a quiet night. Not *Real Hustle* and lasagne quiet, but you know – Bingo. How wrong could it go?

Instead I'm pressed up against a door praying that it will hold shut. I'm trying to jump start my brain, trying to find us a way out of this, trying to work out who we could call or how we can solve this, but nothing's happening. Mind's a blank. Plus I'm feeling really very itchy.

Mitchell

Oh I love this bit. Look at him getting water tipped over his head and his braces snapped back and the look on his face!

238

And that little manager-guy with the weasel moustache. Always looks so cross. Can't remember if I ever knew him. That'd be great, wouldn't it? To say you knew the man who was in those Laurel and Hardy films? Oh wow, they're going to try and get that piano up the stairs again, oh this bit is brilliant. Oh, Denise will adore this…

Annie

I just can't believe this is happening. I don't know what to do. I've no power. It's not like I can blow the vampires away or anything. I can't move. I'm standing here, holding a cup of tea and watching Denise die and George try and fight off the vampires, and I could scream. I kind of blame Denise for all this. Like when you'd find two guys fighting over her. Or when Owen would smirk at me and say 'Denise was looking hot tonight, wasn't she?' I'd wonder what he really meant, and I'd know it wasn't her fault, but I'd somehow blame her for how Owen was, and… I don't know, I just don't know. I just wanted this to be normal. But here we all are again. Waiting for the end of the world.

***

George cried out with fear, feeling the door shake and start to splinter. 'Help me!' he yelled to Mitchell who stood up and sort of strolled over to him.

'What would you like me to do?' he asked dopily.

'Put your weight on this door!' screamed George.

'Oh, that's never going to hold,' sighed Mitchell, and sloughed off to the kitchen. 'Kettle's on,' he called back. 'Want anything?'

'I want to live!' cried George. 'Please! Come back and help

keep this door shut. There's a ravenous army of vampires outside.'

He could hear the shrug in Mitchell's voice. 'Why bother? The back door's wide open.'

'Then shut it!' screamed Annie, tearing through as a darkness swept across the room.

'What the hell?' said George. He turned to see Denise standing next to him.

'Denise!' he said, in a ghastly attempt at bonhomie. 'Hiiiii – how are you feeling?'

'Like death,' said Denise.

'Well, well,' muttered George gamely. 'Soon get you back on your feet. Ambulance on its way. Honestly.'

'What are you doing?'

'Hmmm,' said George, leaning back against the rattling door. 'Well, good point. Keeping out the vampire hordes. Not terribly successfully, because Magnificent Mitchell invited them all in.'

'Oh,' said Denise. 'Bummer.'

'Yes,' replied George, his whole body shaking as the door splintered audibly. 'And I'm trying to hold the letterbox shut with my buttocks, which is quite marvellously firming, and my nose really itches. Not. A. Great. Day.' He smiled.

Denise leaned over him.

'Wh-what are you doing?' asked George, alarmed.

'Relax,' laughed Denise. 'I'm just going to scratch your nose for you.'

'Oh,' George said, smiling back at her. 'Thank you... Thank you. That would be... um, very lovely. Thank you.'

She scratched his nose. 'Better?' she asked.

George considered. 'Not sure, really,' he said. 'Do it again.'

She scratched his nose and then pecked him on the cheek.

Annie came back through. 'Not interrupting anything, am I?'

Denise smiled. 'Not at all. Feel free to rub his nose. Is that tea?'

'You're making tea in a crisis?' asked George.

'Always,' said Annie.

'And that's why I love you,' said Denise. She laughed.

'How are you feeling?' asked Annie. 'Should you be up?' Then she stopped still, staring.

Denise grinned, shaking her head, her hair falling down slowly. 'No, no, definitely not. I feel very, very hung over. And there's a smell... I'm rather afraid it's me. Where's Dr McGough?'

'Out,' said George, a little too quickly. 'Gone out. For more medicine.'

'Really?' said Denise. 'Well, it had better be stronger than this stuff.' She indicated the swaying coat stand by her side.

'What do you mean?' asked George.

She flicked the bag with her finger. 'It's just a saline flush. Oh come on, George, surely you read the label.'

'Oh,' said George, truly alarmed. 'But.. what... I mean, what...'

Denise looked at him, so sadly. 'Sorry,' she said. 'I shouldn't have let on about that, should I?' She looked up and smiled at him, suddenly very young and very brave.

'Look,' she said. 'Sorry – I've had a couple of months to know about this and it's really not so... you know...' She tailed off as she noticed something in the corner of the room.

'That,' she said, 'is a very new door, isn't it?'

'Yes,' said Annie quietly.

'Not there when I went to sleep.'

'No.'

'Funny time to put a new door in.'

'Yes.'

'Thought so.'

'It's there for you.' Annie's voice was gentle.

'I see.' Denise sighed. 'Right then.' She hugged Annie. 'Sorry,' she said. 'Don't let this put you off Bingo.'

Annie clutched at her sadly. 'I won't.'

In a tangle of coat stand and drip cable and hair, Denise walked through the door and waved.

'It's been fun,' she said, and the door closed behind her.

Annie and George just watched in silence for a moment. They couldn't exactly say when the door faded away. But they were aware of the shadows in the room lifting, and Denise's body was revealed, sat in the chair, at peace.

'Well,' said George. 'I guess "sorry" doesn't even begin to—'

'Don't,' said Annie.

They heard Mitchell falling over in the kitchen.

'Jeez,' he gasped. 'That stench! I really don't feel too—'

The next sound was Mitchell throwing up in the sink.

George stood there, the last line of defence between the house and the vampires, looking stunned at the body of Annie's friend, and also wondering, just a little, if Mitchell had bothered to take the cups out of the sink before he'd thrown up.

In the street, the vampires fell back from the door of the house. As McGough watched in amazement, they fell to the ground retching and vomiting, gagging and screaming. He patted the vial in his pocket sadly. He knew what had happened and it didn't give him any pride.

Soon, though, soon they'd be able to refine the effect.

He slipped from behind the bath and ran quickly down the road.

Janice knelt sobbing on the pavement, trying to keep the vomit out of her hair and away from her shoes. This felt like a truly dreadful night, the kind of night that was the reason she'd given up hen parties.

She looked at the group of vampires gathered around her and she suddenly, desperately hated them. She didn't want to lead them. They could look after themselves.

McGough carried on running down the blandly empty street, and turned a corner.

There, leaning for support against a low brick wall, was an elderly couple.

He wanted to run past them, but his instincts came into play. *Always doing good*, he thought ruefully. *I just can't help myself.*

'Are you all right?' he asked.

The little old lady looked up at him, wheezing, and smiled gratefully.

'Just let me get me breath back,' she said, trying for a smile.

The man stepped behind him. 'It's the wife, see,' he said, quite unnecessarily. 'She's had one of her turns. Something in the air…'

'Really?' said McGough weakly, feeling for the test tube in his pocket.

'It's been a funny old evening, hasn't it?' the woman said, leaning on her shopping basket.

'Oh it has indeed,' agreed McGough readily.

'And then along comes a nice gent like you,' said the man, stepping closer still.

'Oh yes, so kind,' said the old lady, leaning closer. 'The answer to our prayers…'

Was She Worth It?

76

Annie sat on the back doorstep, looking out at the twinkling lights of Bristol and listening to the distant sirens. Normal service.

The door opened quietly and George stood over her, smiling nervously. 'Budge up?' he asked.

'Sure,' said Annie, and slid, just slightly, along the cold concrete.

There was an awkward silence.

'You know,' said George eventually, 'this is one of those times when it would be nice if either of us smoked.'

'Yup,' said Annie, looking back out at the city.

'So... the ambulance has taken Denise away,' said George. 'Mitchell will be calling in a favour tomorrow with the coroner. That is, so long as he can convince him that it was nothing to do with vampires.'

'Well, it wasn't. Not technically.' Annie sniffed slightly. 'It

245

was my fault. I couldn't do anything to help her. I couldn't stop anything. Nothing. I'm useless.'

'No,' said George. 'You weren't. It could have been much worse. Really.'

'Yeah.' Annie stared dead ahead, unconvinced. George knew better than to press it.

'It'll be fine. So long as Mitchell can keep his head out of a bucket.'

'Yeah.' Annie brightened slightly. 'Who knew? It was like *The Exorcist*!'

'Don't start getting ideas,' said George. 'I spend all day mopping that kind of thing up. I don't need to practise at home.'

'I'll try my best not to,' said Annie solemnly. 'But I wish I could do the head-swivelling trick.'

'Poor Mitchell.'

'Yeah,' said Annie.

'And I'm sorry. Sorry about your friend. She was nice.'

'Thanks,' Annie nodded. 'Although "she was nice" won't look that impressive on the gravestone.'

George snorted slightly. 'Yes. I guess I'm just not good with the... you know.'

'It's all right,' said Annie, laying a hand on his. 'I know. Thank you.'

'Do you think we could have...? Done... anything?' asked George.

Annie shook her head. 'I'm not really sure... I think that's why she could see me. She already had one foot in the grave when she turned up. But at least she could see me. That was...' She paused carefully. 'She was nice.'

'Yeah,' said George. 'She was nice.'

They sat there for a bit longer.

'Gives you piles, you know,' said George.

'What?'

'Sitting on cold concrete like this.'

Annie smiled, just slightly. 'Ghosts don't get piles.'

'You sure?'

'I'll let you know.'

They sat there for a bit longer.

The next morning, Mitchell made his way slowly and steadily down the hospital corridor, his eyes clamped shut behind his darkest glasses. He'd jammed his headphones in, more to block out the noise than anything else. His entire weight was resting on the mop, his face creased in a look of sheer agony.

'Hiiiiiii,' George appeared in his line of sight.

'Leave me alone,' growled Mitchell.

'I was just dropping by,' said George casually. 'See if you fancied a bacon sandwich?'

Mitchell shuddered.

'Or, you know, just some dry toast and a Red Bull?'

Mitchell tried to shake his head, stopped, and winced.

'Or maybe I should just open a lovely packet of kippers?'

Mitchell stopped, and swallowed with difficulty.

'Coo,' said George. 'You just went paler.'

Mitchell stretched out a hand and grasped George by the throat. 'I feel like I am going to die. Again. When I have finished dying, I will hunt you down and kill you until you're dead. No matter how many fish you stuff in your pockets. Understood?'

'Understood,' said George solemnly. 'I'm just glad to see you're OK. That's all.'

'Sweet,' said Mitchell.

'And hey, maybe it wasn't our best day, but at least neither of us ate anyone.'

'That so?' said Mitchell. 'Rumour in the canteen is that Dr McGough didn't turn up to work this morning.'

'He'll be sadly missed,' said George. 'Although...'

'You're going to mention his cure for vampires, aren't you?' Mitchell looked, if possible, more pained.

'No, no no. Of course not. Well, yes. I mean... Was he doing a good thing?'

Mitchell looked at his hand. 'I dunno. I generally try and examine scientific breakthroughs by whether or not they result in a big pile of dead bodies.'

'OK... but do you think he was right?'

'I don't know,' said Mitchell, and pushed the mop past him down the corridor. Then he paused and turned around. 'Ask me again when I feel human.'

'Yeah,' said George, and watched him go.

Annie walked around the house. She picked up the coat stand and put it back where it belonged. Then she gathered up all the cups of tea from the living room and took them through to the kitchen, pouring them carefully down the sink while the kettle boiled. Then she made more tea.

Later she went through a box under the stairs, stuff that Owen had left behind. Months ago she'd grabbed and burnt handfuls of it, but this morning she sorted through the leftovers. And there, tucked into a copy of a Dan Brown book as a temporary bookmark was the postcard:

Dear Annie (and Owen!)
The island is brilliant. I think I might stay. Having the time of

my life. Wish you were here.
   See you soon,
   Love Denise xxx

Annie read it several times. It still didn't mean much more than that – something scribbled down in a hurried minute by a poolside one morning. She turned it over and looked at the picture of a beach and sunset. When she turned it back over, the words had changed. Now the postcard just read:

Dear Annie
Wish you were here.
See you soon,
Love Denise xxx

Annie slipped the postcard back inside the book, popped it into the box and shut the cupboard under the stairs.

Janice Prescott opened the door to her flat and slipped in. A fly buzzed past her but she ignored it, settling down in a chair opposite her boyfriend Neil.

'What a night!' she exclaimed, idly picking some dried-up vomit out of her hair. 'I'm so glad you didn't come along,' she continued. 'It was a real disappointment on a number of levels. I really need to recharge – can you believe it? I think I spent the night in a doorway. Honestly, and I must look such a state. I was trying so hard, and for a few minutes I think we had a real vision for a way forward… but I think that's all gone now. Honestly – I don't know. Maybe I'm just going to need longer to process what's happened to me. But for a few minutes I really saw a way through the woods, and now, in the cold light of day, I may really need to break away from that and start from the bottom up. But there's lots to unpack from it all. Yeah. Tomorrow is another day.'

She smiled and stood up. 'I think I'm just going to make myself a cup of tea and then slip into bed. You want anything?'

Neil didn't answer.

Neil had been dead for several days.

George slid the empty trolley into the loading bay and then gave a yelp. Standing there was Gavin Foot.

'Hello,' said Gavin.

'Hi,' said George.

'Busy day?'

'Yes. You look terrible.'

Gavin looked down at his rumpled clothes and stained T-shirt. 'Yeah. Funny that. Hung over as hell.'

'Right, I see,' said George and fiddled with the straps on the trolley. 'Goodness. Well, happens to us all.'

Gavin coughed, his voice rattling. 'Yeah. Must have been a really wild night. And the curious thing,' he went on, staring at George, 'is that, according to my editor, I was supposed to have been covering a Bingo night in a sports hall that just so happens to have burnt down.'

'Fancy that,' said George, licking his lips nervously.

'I know,' said Gavin, bitterly. 'But I can't remember a thing about it. They reckon it's shock. My memory could come back at any moment.'

George's eyes slid nervously sideways. 'That's… great. Really great news.'

'Yes,' said Gavin. 'It was in your neck of the woods last night, wasn't it?'

George spread out his hands. 'Well, more or less. I mean,

I think I saw a poster or two for the Bingo, yeah. But not really my scene. No, quiet evening in. *Two Pints* marathon.'

'Didn't hear any fire engines, perhaps?' asked Gavin.

'Well, there's always sirens,' said George. 'I personally tend to block them out. That's the price you pay for living in a thriving urban metropolis.'

'Yes,' said Gavin. 'Quite a night.'

'Would you like a glass of water?' asked George suddenly.

'What?' said Gavin.

'Well, I say glass, it's more a plastic cup, really, but you know, rehydration's the best thing for a hangover. That and resting up with Jeremy Kyle. I'll just –' George indicated nipping back indoors. 'Get you that plastic cup, shall I?'

Gavin nodded, and watched George leave.

George came out a minute later, slightly disappointed that Gavin was still there.

Gavin sipped the water, wincing as he swallowed and staring at George.

George stared back.

Gavin finished the water, placing the cup in George's waiting hand. 'Thank you,' he said. 'I'm not sure I want to remember, you know.'

George nodded. 'Perhaps for the best.'

'I think so,' said Gavin. 'I believe I've realised something. I really am just a weddings and flower shows and openings of second-hand car showrooms kind of person. I'm not interested in the bigger picture. Not any more.'

George smiled slightly and looked down at the empty plastic cup. 'Hospital porter,' he said simply. 'Not like I'm going to fight you for lack of vision.'

'No,' said Gavin sadly. He glanced at his watch. 'Better

get on. There's a christening of quadruplets I have to get to. Can you believe it? Named them after The Beatles. Which is a shame, as the girl gets to be Ringo. But there we go. Where there's life, eh?'

'There's hope,' said George, quietly.

When Gavin had gone he put the used cup neatly in the recycling and got on with the day.

Mitchell knocked on the door labelled Dr McGough.

'Housekeeping,' he said gently. He was holding a bin bag. The office was empty, and he tried to look as casual as possible. He emptied the waste bin first, then went carefully through the paper recycling. Nothing. Then, very quietly and carefully, he opened the filing cabinet.

It was empty. Every single drawer.

He turned round and switched on the computer. After a moment the hard drive ground into silence and a cursor sat there blinking emptily at him. 'Wiped,' he muttered, and stood up, holding his black sack forlornly.

He was about to leave when he noticed something. A framed photograph placed face down on the desk. He turned it up and there was the young McGough, with proper hair and a smile and a wife and a daughter. It was clearly a very old photograph. Mitchell looked at it for a minute and then put it back, face down, and left the office.

Annie made her way gently down the hill. It was a sunny day and the park smelt of bonfires. She stood at the edge of the field, looking at the blackened grass and churned earth where the sports hall had been.

From where she stood on the touchlines, she could see the figures of two little old ladies picking gently through the rubble and ash. From this distance she couldn't see whether they were happy or sad. Or anything much.

She waved, but they didn't see her, just carried on sifting through the ruins. One of them looked up and, for a moment, seemed to see something. Then she shook her head and bent down to work again.

Eventually, Annie turned around and went home.

Back at the house, a hand reached for the doorbell and pressed it.

But there was no one there.

After a while, the woman quietly walked away.

ACKNOWLEDGEMENTS

I'd like to thank Toby Whithouse, Steve Tribe and Albert DePetrillo, plus Simon Guerrier, Mark Michalowski, Lee Binding, Kate Webster and Joseph Lidster, and everyone on set for making us feel so welcome. Oh, and Annie, if you're reading this? We're waiting for you. Soon.

(Nobody wins.)

Also available from BBC Books

being human
THE ROAD

by Simon Guerrier

ISBN 978 1 846 07898 9   £7.99

Annie has learned quite a bit about her new friend Gemma: she's from Bristol, she used to work in a pharmacy, and she's never forgiven herself for the suicide of her teenage son. She also died ten years ago and doesn't know why she's come back through that door...

Perhaps it has something to do with the new road they're building through the rundown part of town. The city's plans are sparking protests, and Annie knows those derelict houses hold a secret in Gemma's past. Will stopping the demolition help Gemma be at peace again? Annie, George and Mitchell get involved in the road protest, but they're more concerned by mysterious deaths at the hospital. Deaths that have also attracted the attention of the new Hospital Administrator...

Featuring Mitchell, George and Annie, as played by Aidan Turner, Russell Tovey and Lenora Crichlow in the hit series created by Toby Whithouse for BBC Television.

Also available from BBC Books

being human
CHASERS

by Mark Michalowski

ISBN 978 1 846 07899 6   £7.99

George's friend, Kaz, arrives at the flat with a staggering request: she and her partner Gail want to have a child, and they'd like George to be the father. George is warming to the idea – he's always wanted kids, and he can be as involved in the baby's life as he wishes – but he is wary: what if his condition is genetic?

Mitchell and Annie don't approve of the new plan, but Mitchell is wrestling with a difficult decision of his own. A patient at the hospital, Leo, is surprisingly good company for a pasty older bloke who believes the 1980s were a golden age. But he seems a little too interested in Mitchell's history – and he has a surprising request of his own in store for his new friend…

Featuring Mitchell, George and Annie, as played by Aidan Turner, Russell Tovey and Lenora Crichlow in the hit series created by Toby Whithouse for BBC Television.